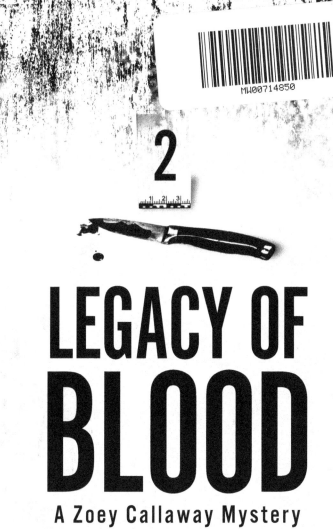

2

LEGACY OF BLOOD

A Zoey Callaway Mystery

DEBI CHESTNUT

MONOCLE

A Cayelle Imprint

LEGACY OF BLOOD

Cayélle Publishing/Monocle Imprint
Lancaster, California USA
www.CayellePublishing.com

Orders by U.S. trade bookstores and wholesalers, contact Freadom Distribution:
Freadom@Cayelle.com

Categories: 1. Mystery   2. Detective   3. Suspense
Printed in the United States of America

Cover Art by Robin Ludwig Design, Inc.
Interior Design & Typesetting by Ampersand Book Interiors

ISBN: 978-1-952404-58-0 [paperback]
ISBN: 978-1-952404-57-3 [ebook]
Library of Congress Control Number 2021935836

laid in bed, pondering whether to go for a run or go back to sleep. My head was pounding from the bottle of wine I'd swilled last night in a moment of self-pity, but I opted for the run. No point in wasting a sunny March morning in Hope Harbor. We didn't get many sunny days in the winter. It was normally dark, gray, and snowy.

After starting a pot of coffee, I checked my email. A few orders had come in from my clients—a credit check from Alba Insurance, a skip tracing order from one of the attorneys in town, and a request for a meeting from the FBI.

Hmm. Wonder what that's about.

They can wait a couple hours.

I threw on a pair of black leggings and a sweatshirt before lacing up my running shoes and heading out the front door. The cold air slapped me in the face as I ran down the porch steps, and a brisk wind was blowing off the lake.

Damn it! Sunny doesn't mean warm.

Halfway down the block, I realized I'd forgotten my cell phone, but decided not to turn back to get it. A five-mile run without music wouldn't kill me.

I started out at a trot to warm up, and pretty soon I'd hit my stride and was flying down the boardwalk next to the waterfront. I waved to Father Alexander as I jogged past him. My neighbor, Bea Perkins, had introduced me to him one day when I'd stopped by the church offices where she worked. She'd gushed like a teenager. I think she liked him, but he was a young priest, and she a matronly woman. Nothing worse than unrequited love. The thought made me chuckle.

A flock of geese had come in off the partially frozen lake, and were waddling around the boardwalk to find a place to rest that had been warmed by the morning sun. They forced me to slow my stride to avoid them, and hissed at me as I tiptoed through them. I could have run around them, but my shoes would have gotten wet in the deep snow that lingered in the grassy areas of the park.

I headed up to the front of the park to cross the street. When I got to the corner, a delivery service van stopped to let me cross. I turned to wave at the driver, but he had his head down and didn't see me.

I was going to go up Main Street, but today traffic was heavy as people shuffled for parking spaces in front of the bakery. Duke Stevens, the owner of the bakery, made fresh cinnamon rolls every morning, and people lined up down the block to get one as they came out of the oven. As I got closer, the aroma of the sweet confections wafted down the sidewalk, and the smell made my stomach growl.

I detoured and ran up a side street. I was in the middle of the block when I heard someone screaming. It wasn't the normal, *Oh, my God. There's a spider*, scream. This was a bloodcurdling scream.

I stopped in my tracks. Two houses up the sidewalk, I saw a young, attractive woman in a chic black dress, standing on a porch. Her large black purse slipped off her shoulder and dropped to the ground.

She raised her hands to her face. "Help!"

I crossed the distance in record time, and as I raced up the steps to her front porch, I saw something laying half-in, half-out of the house. It took me a second to realize it was a woman.

I walked over to the young woman. She'd stopped screaming, and was standing with her arms wrapped around her trembling body.

"Did she fall?"

"No. I don't think so," she said, after it registered that someone was there.

"Okay. Just take a deep breath and calm down." I moved over to the woman who lay prone on the porch.

Maybe she'd been attacked or abused by a significant other, and ran here looking for safety. Maybe she'd crawled here, if she was injured.

No. There were no signs of that in the snow. In fact, the only marks in the snow were where I'd run across the lawn.

She wasn't wearing any shoes. If she'd tried to escape from someone, she left in a hurry. Streaks of blood stained the front of her white sweater, and her black pants were undone and bunched up around her waist, as if she'd dressed in a hurry. Her dark, shoulder-length hair looked wet and was splayed around her head.

It hadn't rained or snowed last night.

I crouched down by her head and realized her hair was soaked in blood. That's when I noticed her throat had been slit with a cut so deep she'd nearly been decapitated.

I straightened and spun my head away to find a stretch of glistening snow to clear my mind of the horrible image. But even then, I knew I had to look again, because I'd glimpsed something odd. A patch of white on her neck.

Eventually I forced my gaze back to the face with the glazed eyes. Yes, the body came with a note. The neat square of paper had been attached to the woman's neck with a large safety pin, the pin woven in and out of the tender skin of her neck. Cruel? Well, it had probably been attached after she'd died, but the callousness, the dismissiveness of this act seemed almost worse than the murder itself.

It was written in elaborate calligraphy: *Adrianna Martinelli, sometimes your past catches up with you.*

I recoiled and clamped my hand over my mouth. My stomach churned. I raced down the porch steps and vomited in the snow.

After wiping my mouth on the sleeve of my sweatshirt, I went back onto the porch to talk to the woman who'd found the body. She was quiet now, but trembling. I couldn't blame her.

I stood in front of her, blocking her view of the body.

"Are you Adrianna?"

She stared at me blankly, my question not registering for a moment.

"Yes." Her voice was shaky.

"I'm Zoey. Did you call 911?"

"No, I just..." She threw her arms around me sobbed on my shoulder.

"It's going to be okay." I extricated myself from her grasp. "Where's your phone?"

She handed me her purse. I turned one of the porch chairs to face away from the body, and gently lowered her into it. Then I opened her purse, took out her cell phone and dialed 911.

Nothing else to do but wait.

Within seconds, sirens pierced the quiet morning air.

I walked over to the chair and kneeled in front of Adrianna.

"Do you know this woman?"

She lifted her head and looked at me. "No. I've never seen her before."

"Did you see the note?"

The sirens were getting closer.

"Yes." Tears ran down her cheeks.

"Do you know what it's talking about?"

"No." She started to sob again. "Why would someone do this to me?"

No one had done anything to her. Well, except put a body on her porch. It was the poor woman lying dead that'd had something done to her.

My mind shifted into overdrive. *So she claims the body of a woman she doesn't know is dumped on her porch with a note addressed to her, and she doesn't have a clue who would do something like that, or what it's about? Yeah, right. Oh, well. Not my problem. The police will find out the truth.*

"Okay. The police are almost here. They're going to have a lot of questions. Just tell them the truth, okay?" I took her shaking hands in mine.

Before she could answer, three police cars, an ambulance, and Jason Brock's truck screeched to a halt in front of the house.

Why is Jason here?

He was an FBI agent. They normally don't get involved in local crime.

After the witch cemetery murders last fall, we'd started to date. Everything was hot and heavy for a while, but both of us had built walls around our hearts from previous relationships. Not to mention, Jason had become possessive and a bit too controlling for my liking. So the last time we went out, I told him I thought we should cool it down for a bit. Take things slower. He became enraged and stormed out of my house. That was the last time I'd spoken to him. Until now.

Jason and a man I didn't recognize walked up the porch steps, and I rose to greet them.

"What are you doing here?" Jason set his jaw—a clear sign he wasn't happy.

"I was jogging, and heard someone scream," I said.

"You know her?" the other man said to Jason, and nodded toward me.

"Yes," Jason sighed. "She's Zoey Callaway. Zoey, meet Nate Emerson, the new Hope Harbor homicide detective."

I extended my hand. "Nice to meet you."

He shook my hand with a firm grip. His touch sent tingles through my body, and I pulled my hand away.

"You, too," he said. "Do you live here?"

"She doesn't." Jason scowled. "She lives across the street from me. Just has a nasty habit of turning up anywhere there's a dead body."

Nate gave Jason a quizzical look, and I felt my face redden.

"I-it's not like that," I said. "Can I go now?"

"I may have more questions." Detective Emerson brushed past me and knelt down to examine the body.

His face clouded over when he saw the note.

He got to his feet and walked over to Adrianna. I tried to see what was going on, but the police officers were blocking my view.

The crime scene personnel shooed us off the porch so they could start processing the area. I stepped down the stairs to the front yard. Jason followed me, and we watched the coroner's van pull up behind his truck.

I turned to face him, crossing my arms. "What the hell is wrong with you?"

He met my glare with one of his own. "Just go home and stay out of this. If Nate has any more questions, he can come to you!"

Before I could answer, TV news trucks began to show up in front of the house.

"Go! Now!" Jason said.

I didn't need to be told twice. The last thing I wanted was to get caught by the reporters who'd started to circle around like sharks in a feeding frenzy.

As much as I wanted to take off like a shot to get out of there, I didn't want to draw attention to myself. So I forced myself to stroll down the sidewalk until I was a few houses away, and then broke into a sprint.

On the way home, I replayed the grotesque scene in my head, over and over. I didn't want to forget anything.

I let myself in, ran down the hall to my office, and turned on the TV mounted above my desk. So far, the reporters were still milling around. The cameramen were panning the scene, and I watched closely. Didn't see any sign of Jason, Adrianna, or Detective Emerson. They must have gone into the house.

A white sheet was covering the body of the poor young woman. Who was she? More importantly, why was there a note addressed to Adrianna with the body? Adrianna had to know, or at least have a suspicion. Maybe it had to do with an ex-boyfriend or ex-husband. It could have been that she'd had a lesbian affair, and the boyfriend or husband murdered her.

At any rate, a killer is not going to leave a note about someone's past catching up to them if they've done nothing to them.

I opened a blank word-processing document and started to type in everything I'd witnessed at Adrianna's house. After a half-hour, I sat back, satisfied with my progress.

As much as I wanted to ponder the events of the morning, I had work to do. I kept my attention on the TV as I processed my work orders and completed a few background checks for Alba Insurance. I answered the email from the FBI agreeing to a meeting, and asked for details.

I sat back in my chair to stretch, and glanced up the TV just in time to see Detective Emerson coming down the porch steps, toward the reporters. Jason accompanied him and stood in stoic silence at his side.

"I am Detective Nate Emerson of the Hope Harbor Police Department. Next to me is Special Agent Jason Brock, with the FBI. He has offered the assistance of the Bureau, if needed. I have a short statement, and I will not be taking questions at this time.

"At approximately seven-thirty this morning, we received a 911 call about a body being found on the front porch of a residence. As of right now, we don't have the identity of the victim. This is a very fluid situation. More details will be released when we have them. I caution you against harassing the homeowner. Please respect their privacy. That's all I have for you at this time. Thank you."

Wow, that was impressive. He said a lot without saying anything. They must teach classes in that at the police academy.

While I'd been watching the news, Karma had jumped off my desk and wandered out of my office. I heard her start to meow, and got up to see what had offended her kitty constitution this morning.

As I headed into the kitchen to get more coffee, through the living room window I saw Bea Perkins, my neighbor, walking up the front steps, holding a bakery box.

How does Karma always seem to know when someone is bringing her a treat?

I detoured into the living room and opened the front door for Bea. We exchanged greetings, and she limped past me, into the kitchen. Her knee must have been bothering her again.

While she was dishing out cinnamon rolls from the bakery and getting herself a cup of coffee, I filled her in on the morning's activities. She listened politely, but seemed distracted.

"That's nice, dear." She poured herself a cup of coffee.

"Nice! But it was a murder, Bea." I plopped down in a chair at the table.

"Yes, you said that. I'm sure the police will figure it out." She tapped her nails against the side of her coffee cup.

I sat back in my chair. "What do you think about the note the killer left? I mean, it was safety-pinned to the poor woman's skin."

"That's dreadful!" She shook her head. "What's this world coming to?"

Something wasn't right. Normally, Bea would be eating up all the details and asking a ton of questions. Perhaps a gruesome murder isn't the best choice for breakfast conversation.

No, that hasn't bothered her before. Something's not right in her world.

"Are you okay? Is something wrong, Bea?"

She stabbed a piece of roll with her fork. "Oh, it's that damn Mary Watkins."

"Who's she?"

"She's in the Mavens of Mayhem. You know, my mahjong group," she said, between chews. "She had her genealogy done, and found out she's descended from some earl, I think she said. From England."

I hid a smile. "Okay, and?"

Bea dropped her fork onto her empty plate. "And she's lording it over everyone! Claiming to be a royal. As if. The only thing she's being is a royal pain in the ass. I need you to help me."

"Help you do what?" I got up to pour us more coffee.

I need you to trace my ancestors and find someone who can trump her earl." She put her elbows on the table and stared at me. "I remember my grandmother telling me we descended from someone important, but I can't, for the life of me, remember the details. It was years ago. I'm planning to go to a genealogy seminar at the college given by one of the history professors. Rodger Frost is his name.

"That sounds like a good idea. Maybe he'll trace someone down for you. Of course, if he can't, I'll help you. We can do it together. It'll be fun."

"Oh, poo." Bea slumped in her chair like a deflated balloon. "I don't have a computer, and I can barely operate the one at the church. Please, Zoey?" She looked at me with pleading eyes.

"Okay, I'll go with you. But only after you attend the seminar. You'll have to write down everything you know. Parents, grand-parents, dates, places, and so on. At least give me some place to start," I sighed.

She flashed a broad smile and leapt out of her chair and gave me a hug.

"You're the best, Zoey! I'll get to work right away. I think I have some old papers and stuff in the attic. I'll get everything to you by morning."

And with that, she was gone. I crossed my arms on the table and put my head down on top of them.

"Why, why, why am I such a sucker?"

I got up from the table and tossed back the cold dregs of my coffee. Gave the kitchen island a perfunctory wipe-down, then headed for my office. An email had come in from the FBI saying they wanted to meet this afternoon, and gave me an address in Detroit.

Peachy. All I needed now was to be fired.

While only about fifteen miles away, traffic in downtown Detroit can be brutal, no matter what time of day it is, so I planned to leave early.

I sent out bills to my clients, took a shower, and straightened out the house. As I fluffed up the pillows on the sectional, I saw a police car pull into my driveway. Detective Emerson got out and headed to the porch.

I opened the door for him. "Come in, Detective."

"Thanks." He entered and looked around.

Karma zoomed down the hallway and scaled her cat tree by the front door. She stopped inches from the detective's head and stared at him.

He reached up and caressed her soft fur, and she made happy chirping noises, and contorted her body to give him maximum access.

I shook my head and went into the kitchen. "Coffee?"

"Please." He followed me and settled onto one of the bar stools at the island. "Sorry about not calling first, but I need to ask you some questions about this morning."

It's been my experience that every time someone says something and then adds the word *but*, it means *Ignore everything I just said. Here's what I really mean.*

I sat a large mug of coffee in front of him, along with some creamer, sugar, and a spoon, just in case.

"Now, Miss Callaway," he dumped two sugars into his mug, "how did you come to be at Miss Martinelli's house this morning?"

I sighed. "First, please call me Zoey. And ending up there was not on my agenda. I don't even know her."

He raised an eyebrow. "Go on."

I told him everything I could remember about hearing Adrianna scream, finding the body, and calling the police. As I talked, he took notes in a small black notebook.

"Why did you leave when I told you I'd have more questions?"

"When the reporters showed up, Jason told me to get out of there, so I did."

He nodded.

"Did you identify that poor woman yet?"

"We did. But we're not releasing her name until we notify her family." He drained his coffee.

My mind drifted back to the ugly scene on Adrianna's porch this morning.

"There wasn't enough blood." I refilled our cups.

He went to put some sugar into his coffee, but paused in mid-air. "Excuse me?"

"I'm just saying that if you slit someone's throat like that, you're going to hit the jugular. There would be blood everywhere. There wasn't. In fact, I didn't see any blood at all. So obviously there's another crime scene. Did you find it?"

"Ahh. Now I see what Jason was talking about."

"I'm sorry?" I could feel my blood starting to boil.

What had Jason told him?

He got up from the stool and started toward the front door. I followed and opened it for him.

"Just one more thing," he said. "What exactly is your relationship with Jason Brock?"

The question took me aback.

"Personal or professional reasons, Detective?" I looked up at him through veiled lashes.

His lips parted in a small smile, and he had the decency to blush.

"A little of both, to be honest. Call me Nate. I just don't want to run into conflict-of-interest issues."

"You'll have to ask him."

Truth be told, I wasn't sure what our relationship was.

He nodded, moved out on the porch, and turned to look at me. "I'll be in touch."

"I look forward to it." I shut and locked the door, then hurried to get ready to leave for my meeting with the FBI.

The GPS in my Jeep led me to what, at first glance, seemed to be an abandoned building just outside of downtown. I'd never understood why, when it came to me working for them, every-thing was always so hush-hush. But they paid well, and the work was interesting.

I got out of my truck and surveyed the building. It stood two-stories tall, with few windows. The dull gray paint was peeling off the cinderblocks on the outside of the building, and there was a reinforced steel door straight ahead of me.

I tried to open it, but it was locked.

Am I early? I glanced at my cell phone and saw I was right on time, but I didn't see any other cars in the small parking lot.

Then I heard a deadbolt click, and the door opened halfway to reveal Agent Phillips, my FBI contact.

"Come in, Zoey." He scanned the area outside.

I moved past him, and he shut and locked the door behind me. "This way."

The inside of the building was a sharp contrast to the outside. It was clean, modernized, and filled with bright fluorescent lights.

Phillips led me down a hallway to a conference room and stood back to let me enter first. A large, cheap conference table and six chairs took the center of the room. A telephone had been placed in the center of the table.

He held out my chair and sat next to me.

"Sorry about all the intrigue. But for your own safety, it's important that no one connects you to the FBI. And this meeting never took place. Do you understand?"

I nodded. "What's this about?"

"We're trying to clear up some cold cases. Jane and John Does, unsolved cases, and so forth." He reached in his pocket to pull out an SD card in a plastic case, and sat it on the table in front of me. "This card contains all the information you need for each case. We want you to take the information and do forensic DNA tracking to find or identify the people we're looking for. The DNA for each case has been uploaded into a gene matching database. One of the few that allows law enforcement to match the DNA we have with other people's DNA in the database without a warrant. Understand?"

I nodded.

My mind was spinning. This was cutting-edge stuff! Ever since the Golden Gate Killer had been caught, using this technique, it was becoming more popular. But not without controversy.

"Good." His face relaxed. "We understand this is going to take a considerable amount of time, and we don't expect instant results. But you have the skills to do this type of work, and we prefer for it to be outsourced."

"I understand."

It made sense. They didn't want anything I was doing to be traced back to them.

He pulled a small notebook out of his black suitcoat pocket, tore out a page, and retrieved a pen from his shirt pocket. He wrote something down on the paper and slid it in front of me. It was a number. A large number with a dollar sign in front of it.

I coughed to stifle a gasp.

"This is how much the Bureau is willing to pay you per year. You will be paid monthly instead of by project. Is this number agreeable to you?"

"Yes, it's more than enough."

I'd never made close to that much money before.

"Good. All other work with the Bureau will cease so you can work on this project. I will still be your only contact, and we will continue to exchange information as we normally do." Phillips got up from his chair, indicating the meeting was over.

I tucked the SD card, and the piece of paper with my salary on it, into my bag. As we strode down the hall toward the exit, I recalled something odd I wanted to ask him about.

I pulled out my cell phone and opened a file.

"Do you know what this is? I found it on my phone yesterday, when I did a routine scan."

Agent Phillips took my phone and looked at the app.

"It's exclusive FBI spyware. It allows us to trace a suspect without their knowledge. How did this end up on your phone?" A look of concern crossed his face.

"No idea! But I'd like you to remove it."

Damn right I had an idea. It could only be one person—Jason was tracking my whereabouts.

My blood boiled.

Phillips took my phone and began to fiddle with it. He kept it out of my view so I couldn't see what he was doing.

"It takes a special passcode to uninstall it."

Thanks." I sighed.

I was so mad at Jason I wanted to scream.

"Here you go," Phillips said, a couple minutes later, and handed me the phone.

He opened the steel door and looked out before allowing me to move past him.

"Thank you," I said.

As I maneuvered my Jeep onto the entrance ramp to the freeway, I thought about the meeting and the complex project I'd just taken on. I worried that I'd have to give up my other clients to work on this project, and I wasn't sure I wanted to do that.

Maybe I could do both. The extra money would really help. Owning an older home was more expensive than I'd ever imag-

ined, and as much as I'd loved my Uncle Felix, he'd been neglect-
ful when it came to maintenance.

So far, I'd updated the first floor. Then right before Christmas,
the furnace died and needed to be replaced, along with the central
air. While I had a nice nest egg due to Felix's life insurance policy,
it was still a hit to the finances. No doubt, this job was a windfall.
But what was I going to do about Jason?

Traffic was light, and I made good time getting back to town.
On the way home, I stopped by the office supply store and picked
up some colored file folders and labels. I didn't know how many
I'd need, so I bought the jumbo packs. One can never have too
many file folders.

I pulled into my driveway and unloaded the Jeep. I'd just sat
the bags down on the kitchen island, when Bea came in, carrying a banker's box.

"Here's the stuff from the attic, on my family." She sat the box
down on a bar stool. "I haven't been through it, so Lord knows
what's in here."

"Okay. Thanks." I shrugged out of my coat and hung it up in
the front closet.

Bea busied herself in the kitchen, making coffee.

"So when's that genealogy seminar?" I said.

"Saturday, at one." She struggled to get into one of the high
stools at the island. "So who was that handsome man in the police
car, who was here this morning?"

"The new homicide detective, Nate Emerson." I sat on one of
the stools and sighed.

Nate was Jax's replacement. I wished he hadn't moved back
to Oklahoma. He'd become a good friend, and had helped me
through Uncle Felix's death. I guess he needed a long convales-
cence, maybe even post-traumatic stress counseling after Seth

shot him. Can't be easy finding out the man you worked beside in Homicide was a serial killer.

"I really miss Jax," I said.

"I'm sure you do, dear." Bea reached across the island to pat my hand. "He was a good man. But you've been seeing Jason, haven't you?"

I shrugged. "Kind of. We had a fight. He was getting too clingy."

Clingy? Now that was putting it mildly. And now tracking my movements?

"Well, maybe the sexy new detective will put a spring in your step." She smiled. "Well, I'm sure you have things to do. I have to get back to the church. Talk later, dear." She headed for the door.

"Bye." I waved, but she was already out the door.

I rinsed out the cups and put them in the dishwasher. Then I retrieved the SD card out of my bag, grabbed the bags from the office supply store, and headed into my office. I spent the rest of the afternoon going through all the files on the SD, and making folders for them—red folders for the criminals, and blue for the Jane/John Does. By the time I'd finished, there were well over a hundred files stacked on my desk.

I tried to make room in my file cabinet for all of them, but that was an exercise in futility. I jumped online to order a four-drawer file cabinet, and asked that it be delivered tomorrow. Then I started to read all the case files.

At 5:30, I sat back in my chair and stretched. I'd only made it through twenty case files. There were so many, and each one was urgent. I felt overwhelmed, and wasn't sure where to start.

I felt bad for the families who were still searching for their loved ones, while the criminals were free to commit more crimes.

Karma, who'd been napping on the corner of my desk, on her blanket, stood and engaged in a long, luxurious stretch before looking at me and meowing loudly. It was her dinner time.

We both headed for the kitchen. Karma jumped up on the kitchen counter and sat, waiting. I opened a can of food and dumped it in her dish before refilling her pink water bowl. The aroma of her cat food made my stomach growl, reminding me that I hadn't eaten since breakfast.

I didn't feel like cooking, so I put on my coat and walked the two blocks downtown. Gil's Diner was wedged between the Hope Harbor Historical Society Museum and Dixon's bookstore. The enticing smell of grilled hamburgers greeted me when I walked through the door. The place was packed, and I looked around for a place to sit.

Tabby, one of my favorite waitresses, saw me come in and waved me to a small booth in the back. I ordered a pop and pulled my cell phone out of my purse to check my voicemail.

I was so engrossed in listening to my messages that I jumped when Jason plopped down in the seat across from me. I hadn't even seen him come into the restaurant. He snickered as I tucked my phone back into my bag.

We exchanged greetings and gave our orders to Tabby when she delivered our drinks. Jason unwrapped his straw and dunked it into his pop.

"Did Nate talk to you today?"

"He stopped by. Yes." I arranged a napkin on my lap.

"Good. Now you can leave things alone. You've done your duty."

Before I could reply, Tabby delivered our food, and we spent a minute or two putting condiments on our hamburgers.

"Look, I get you're trying to keep me safe, and I appreciate it. But you have to stop trying to control everything I do. It's not like we're in a committed relationship or anything." I took a big bite of my hamburger.

Jason looked up from his plate, and our gazes locked.

"You're right. We're not in a committed relationship." He scowled. "And I'm not controlling."

I wiped my mouth with my napkin. "Bullshit! You're still tracking my phone."

"No, I'm not." He blushed.

"Oh, come one, Jason. I have a degree in computer forensics, remember? I found the hidden app you put on my phone. An application, by the way, that's only used by the FBI. Agent Phillips removed it for me."

Jason hung his head. "I'm sorry, Zoey."

I took some money and put it on the table, gathered my coat and bag, and stood.

"Sometimes sorry isn't enough, Jason."

Without even looking at him again, I walked out of the restaurant and headed home.

I worked on the FBI files until a little after 1:00 a.m., and then crawled into bed.

3

The morning was crisp and cold. A stiff wind was blowing in off the frozen lake, and a light snow had started to fall as I finished up my five-mile run. I popped into Gil's to grab a coffee to-go, then walked the rest of the way home.

I turned on the TV to catch the morning news. A reporter, who was wearing too much makeup, was standing on the sidewalk in front of Adrianna Martinelli's house. She said the woman who'd been murdered was Sienna Blackwell, and that the police had few leads in her death.

As she talked, I retrieved a pen and paper from the kitchen and wrote down the murder victim's name. The reporter went on to say that Sienna Blackwell had been an elementary school teacher, single, and had lived in Southfield.

Hmm.

Southfield was about forty miles west of Hope Harbor. How did she end up way out here?

The newscast then switched back to the anchor, who reported on a traffic delay because of a delivery van that had burned on the freeway in Detroit, early that morning.

I clicked off the TV, and after my shower, headed into my office to tackle the mound of work piled up on my desk. I was just digging into the first file when Karma showed up at my office door and gave a loud meow, before casting a glance toward the living room.

Something was up. I sighed and walked down the hallway to see the office supply truck backing into my driveway.

"You're almost better than a guard dog." I stroked her soft fur.

She climbed up onto her cat tree and stared as the delivery men wheeled my new filing cabinet into the house, on a dolly. They set it in place for me and left after I signed for the delivery.

So much for getting anything done this morning. It was going to take some time to arrange all the files in the cabinet the way I wanted them.

By early afternoon, everything was put away, and I'd spent a couple hours working on one of the cases. While I'd used the DNA matching database before, it had been a couple years. So there was going to be a sharp learning curve before I had it mastered.

I printed out the user's manual, three-hole punched the pages, and put them into a binder that I'd labeled with the name of the program. It was always such a pain to stop in the middle of doing something and have to switch screens, so having the printed manual would make things easier—I hoped.

As much as I tried to focus on the task at hand, my mind kept wandering back to the poor woman who'd been murdered. I set the FBI file aside and switched databases to run a quick background check on Sienna Blackwell.

Her finances were in order. She'd never even had a parking ticket. And by all accounts, her life seemed pretty average. Even a check of her social media accounts turned up nothing of interest. But then again, I wasn't sure what I was looking for.

I did the same for Adrianna. After all, the note pinned to that poor woman's neck had been addressed to her.

Had Sienna just been a way to deliver a message to Adrianna? It sure seemed that way to me. The thought broke my heart.

Adrianna's background report was a little more interesting. She was doing okay financially, and nothing jumped out at me at first glance. She'd earned an associate degree at Ferris State, in Big Rapids, Michigan, and was working as a paralegal for a large law firm in Detroit. She was making decent money.

I found her resume on a job search site, and discovered that she changed jobs a lot. Her background check also revealed that she moved frequently—every two years or less. That would explain the frequent job changes. But why?

After saving a picture of both Adrianna and Sienna to my computer, I printed them out and wheeled the large whiteboard into the middle of my office. I chuckled as I remembered Jason calling it my *murder board.*

I put Adrianna and Sienna's pictures on the board, and wrote down all the other information on index cards. Once I had put them in their appropriate places on the board, I stood back to study my handywork.

Nothing. I had nothing. No suspects. No motive. Just a bunch of facts that didn't make any sense.

Karma had come into my office and perched on my desk, staring at me. She sat and stared at the board, twitched her ears, then looked at me and blinked.

"I know." I leaned against my desk, beside her. "We're obviously missing a few pieces of the puzzle."

She meowed her response, jumped off my desk and disappeared down the hallway.

I glanced at the clock hanging on my office wall. It was almost 6:00. No wonder I was hungry.

I fed Karma, then ran a quick brush through my hair and put it up in a neat ponytail, before donning my parka and boots. A few minutes later, I pulled up into Adrianna's driveway.

Her car was there. She was home.

She must have been watching, because she opened the door before I had a chance to ring the doorbell.

"Zoey, right?" She gave me a half-smile.

"Yes. How are you?"

She stepped out of the way to let me enter.

"I'm doing okay. So glad you stopped by. I never got a chance to thank you the other day."

I followed her into the sparsely furnished living room.

"No thanks necessary." I smiled.

As I looked around, I couldn't help but notice that there was nothing personal. No pictures, no cutesy girl stuff, nothing. The room looked generic, impersonal, like it was all staged.

"I was wondering if you wanted to grab a bite to eat at Gil's?" I said. "I hate to eat alone."

"Oh, I'd love to!" Her face lit up. "I haven't lived here that long, and I don't have any friends outside of co-workers. Let me get my coat."

Well, that was the truth. According to what I'd found online, she'd only been renting this house for about two months.

We drove separately, and ended up sitting in a cozy booth not far from the front door. After placing our orders, I looked up at her expectantly.

"The police think I'm lying." Her eyes teared up, and she wiped them with a napkin.

"About what?"

"They think I should know who left that poor woman on my porch." She placed her forearms on the table and folded her hands. "But I don't."

"I think what they want to know is who did you piss off?" I took a sip of pop. "An ex-boyfriend, ex-husband. An old co-worker, maybe?"

"No one." She avoided my gaze.

Yeah, right.

I sat back in the booth and glared at her. "Adrianna, there isn't a person alive who hasn't pissed someone off. It's a fact of life. To say that you've never pissed anyone off can't possibly be the truth."

She opened her mouth to say something, but thought better of it. While I waited for her to respond, I saw Nate Emerson walk in. He saw who I was with and raised an eyebrow before sitting at one of the high-top chairs at the bar.

"Well, I do have a couple of old boyfriends. But I can't imagine any of them doing something like that." She shook her head.

Realizing I wasn't going to get anything else out of her, I gave up for the moment. Better to befriend her before pushing harder. Maybe then she'd trust me enough to tell me what was really going on.

I changed the subject, and we spent the rest of the evening talking about our jobs, men, and our lives. We paid the bill, then left the restaurant, arm in arm, and hugged when we got outside.

As Adrianna hurried to her car, I noticed her head on the swivel.

Interesting. What was she afraid of?

I drove home and got into my pajamas. I felt like a slug, I'd eaten so much. Maybe I'd have to push for that sixth mile tomorrow just to work off the hamburger and ice cream brownie dessert.

Karma followed me into my bedroom and jumped on the bed to get comfortable. As I plugged in my cell phone to charge, I noticed I'd missed a call. It was Nate. I smiled, knowing why he'd called.

"You're just going to have to wait, Detective." I crawled into bed and turned off the light.

It was only 8:30, but I was exhausted.

When I got back from my run the next morning, Nate was waiting for me on the front porch. I trotted up the steps, and he handed me a large coffee. Bless that man.

I unlocked the door, and he followed me inside.

"So?" He sat at the kitchen island.

As I sat next to him, I noticed he was wearing black cowboy boots.

Where'd he come from?

"So what?" I gave him a coy smile.

He shook his head and snickered. "Adrianna."

"Oh, that. Nothing really."

I filled him in on my conversation with her last night.

"She's hiding something," I said.

"That was my feeling, too. Keep working at it."

"I'm sorry?" I got up from my chair and started to pace around the kitchen.

His gaze followed me.

"You want my help?"

"It makes sense." He shrugged. "She's more likely to open up to another woman more than to a man. Especially a cop."

He had a point.

I stopped pacing and pondered his request. Jason would be furious. But did he have to know?

"I'll see what I can do." I smiled.

Nate drained his coffee and got up from his stool. He deposited the empty cardboard cup into the garbage and walked over to where I was standing.

"I have to get to work," he said.

I followed him to the front door and opened it. "Stay safe."

He caressed the side of my face. "Thanks. I will."

Then he was gone.

I put my hand to my cheek where he'd touched me, and stared after him, confused. I barely knew him, but the touch seemed so intimate.

I shook my head and locked the door behind me.

Karma and I retreated to my office, and I spent the morning trying to identify a rapist, using his DNA. It didn't take long to realize this project was a lot harder than I thought it would be, and was going to consume a huge amount of time. But the pay was good, and I thoroughly enjoyed the thrill of the hunt. Good thing they weren't expecting immediate results.

By noon, my eyes were burning and red from staring at the computer screen, but I'd made some progress and felt I was getting close. I stretched as I walked into the kitchen to see what I could find for lunch. The almost-empty refrigerator reminded me it had been a long time between grocery shopping trips.

"Damn it!" I slammed the refrigerator shut.

I got bundled up and drove the few short miles to the store. An hour later, I pulled back into my driveway with way too much food. I should have known not to go to the grocery store hungry.

I grabbed a handful of bags and dumped them on the kitchen island. As I turned around to go get more, Jason came in with the rest of the groceries.

"What did Nate want this morning?" He put the bags on the counter.

As I busied myself putting away the food, I thought about how much—or little—I wanted to tell him. Better to play it safe and say as little as possible.

"Oh, he saw me with Adrianna Martinelli at Gil's last night and wanted to know if she told me anything useful."

Jason plopped down on one of the stools. "Why did you have dinner with Adrianna last night?" His tone was measured.

"I just wanted to make sure she was okay. After all, it's not every day you find a dead body on your porch." I tried to sound casual and shrug it off as no big deal.

He shook his head. "Why not just tell me the truth and say you were fishing for information? I know you, Zoey."

I slammed the pantry door shut and whirled around to face him.

"Maybe you don't know me as well as you think you do. Did it ever occur to you that maybe, just maybe, I was just trying to be a friend to her? She's been through a horrible experience."

My mom always said the best defense is a good offense.

"If it was anybody else, yes!"

I leaned against the pantry door and put my hands to my face to calm myself.

"I don't want to fight anymore, Jason. This is how I am. Take it or leave it. If you can't handle it, then I don't see any point in continuing our relationship. If that's what it is."

He stared at me for a few moments, then got up from the stool, and before he stepped out the front door, turned to look at me.

"All I want is to keep you safe. I love you, Zoey."

He shut the door behind him.

4

I stood and stared after him. It had never dawned on me that he felt that way, considering how rude and bossy he'd been towards me lately.

But how did I feel about him? I cared for him, yes. But love?

That question, I couldn't answer.

After devouring a tuna fish sandwich that I ended up sharing with Karma, I went back to work. It was after midnight before I stopped and shut off my computer. I had managed to track down relatives of the rapist, and typed out a report with all the information the FBI should need.

I'd text Agent Phillips in the morning. It was late, and he—unlike me—might actually have a life.

Bea came over right after I got back from my morning run, with cinnamon rolls from the bakery. She prattled on about the genealogy talk we would be attending that afternoon. Thank goodness she did, because I had forgotten about it.

We settled down at the kitchen table.

"So you had quite a parade of men through here yesterday."

"Huh?" I gave her a blank stare.

Bless her heart for being my nosy neighbor. It showed that she cared.

"That cute new detective, and Jason." Her tone sounded disapproving.

The thought amused me.

"Yes. So many men, so little time." I let out a mock sigh, putting the back of my hand on my forehead.

"That's not even funny." She let her fork clatter onto her plate. "Really, Zoey."

I realized I had offended her sensitive disposition.

"I'm sorry, Bea. I was kidding. Nate stopped by to find out about my conversation with Adrianna. And Jason came over to tell me he loved me." I sat back in my chair, waiting for that little bombshell to sink into her brain.

"He actually said that?" She gave me a broad smile. "Oh, that's wonderful!" She clapped in delight.

"Glad you're happy." I turning my attention back to my breakfast.

A look of concern crossed her face. "You don't love him? How could you not love him? He's adorable."

Bea was heading down a road I wasn't ready to travel, so I changed the subject to the impending genealogy seminar.

"Have you made any progress with my family?" she said.

I got up from the table and started to clear the dishes.

"Honestly, Bea, I haven't even had time to look at anything."

I spent a few minutes telling her about my new assignment from the FBI. She listened and then got up from the table.

"That's fabulous news! I'll see you about noon. Can you drive?"

I assured her I would drive, and walked her to the door.

After she had left, I texted Agent Phillips: *Mabel has a package for you.*

He texted back that he'd be there in forty-five minutes, and that Mabel had a message for me as well.

As I took my shower, I couldn't help but wonder whether the entire FBI was so cloak and dagger, or whether it was just Agent Phillips. I couldn't send him emails or files, even if they were encrypted. There was virtually no way to connect him with me. Why was he so paranoid?

None of the work I was doing for him could be considered top secret or dangerous.

As I rinsed the conditioner out of my hair, I decided it was Agent Phillips who was so paranoid. I'd done work for the FBI before he came along, and it was nothing like this. When I worked for another agent a couple years ago, everything was done through encrypted email. Was Agent Phillips running some type of personal agenda?

I wrapped myself in a fluffy towel and went to my bedroom. Karma was sitting on the bed, watching me.

"And another thing." I looked at her. "Why do we have to always meet in strange places?"

She yawned and stretched before curling up for her morning nap.

"You're no help." I dislodged her to make the bed.

After getting dressed, I dashed out the door to meet Agent Phillips. Our normal meeting place was at Oakmont Cemetery, on 24 Mile Road. It was a large cemetery flanked by older homes to the sides, and a new subdivision along the back separated by a wrought iron fence.

I pulled into the graveyard and turned to right on the narrow road that ran around the perimeter of the cemetery. When I got back to the front, I parked by the black wrought-iron fence. Pulled the envelope out of my bag and placed it on the grave of Mabel Dunham, then retreated to my truck.

Out of my windshield, I could see the entrance of the cemetery. A few minutes passed before Agent Phillips pulled in and parked by the white groundskeeper's building not too far from the entrance, then walked over to Mabel's grave.

Her grave marker was carved out of marble and shaped like a bed, complete with a headboard, sideboards, and a footboard. Growing inside the *bed* was lily of the valley.

Phillips crouched down and laid a bouquet of flowers against the headstone. When he stood, I saw him tuck the envelope inside his jacket. He looked around the cemetery before heading back to his car. Without even a glance in my direction, he pulled away.

"That's strange. He's never left flowers before. Was that the message he mentioned in his text?"

I walked over to Mabel's grave, knelt down to pick up the flowers, and examined the bouquet. They were from the local grocery store. Nothing special. Then I saw the edge of a piece of paper sticking out from the middle of the stems halfway down the bouquet, and plucked it out of the cellophane.

In his neat hand, Agent Phillips had written, *Be careful.*

"Now what the hell does that mean?"

I replaced the flowers, but kept the note. As much as I wanted to text him and ask him what he meant, I knew better. He wouldn't answer. He'd told me once that I was on a need-to-know basis, and evidently I didn't need to know. Maybe it had something to do with the whole Adrianna matter. After all, Jason and Agent Phillips worked in the same office. Or could it be that the work I was doing was more dangerous than he'd let on?

After returning home, I worked on a Jane Doe file until it was time to pick up Bea and go to the seminar. Traffic was light, and we arrived early at the community college. Bea picked out seats for us center stage, second row. As we got settled, she pulled a pen and pad out of her voluminous purse.

The auditorium filled up quickly. Apparently, Tracing Your British Ancestors was a hot topic. A woman introduced the speaker, Rodger Frost, and a round of applause broke out. A large man, probably in his early forties, walked across the stage. His light brown hair was cut military style, and he spoke in a clipped British accent, his voice deep but pleasant. He was much younger than I thought he would be, but seemed extremely knowledge-able about his subject matter.

Bea was scribbling notes on her pad, while I just sat back and listened. Most of what he was talking about I already knew, but it was still nice to have up-to-date information about new tools and databases available to genealogists.

Two hours later, when he'd finished speaking, many of the people in the audience rushed the stage to speak with him. Of course, Bea was among them. I followed at a slower pace and stayed in the background while people asked their questions, amazed at how patient he was in answering them and offering assistance.

Bea rushed over to me. "Zoey, come here!" She grabbed my arm and dragged me toward Professor Frost. "This is the girl I was telling you about. She's going to help me."

I introduced myself, and we shook hands.

"A pleasure. Here, take my card and let me know if you need any help." He handed me a business card.

After thanking him, I ushered Bea out of the auditorium before she attempted to monopolize all of his time.

"See, it's not that hard," I said, once we were on the way home.

"Oh, shush." Bea waved a hand. "I barely understood a word he said. What, with parish records and all that other stuff he was talking about. Please, Zoey, you have to help me."

"I will." I gave her a sideways glance. "It's going to be a while, though, so give me time." *Damn! I thought by coming with her, it would get me out of this.*

She agreed, and I pulled into my driveway and helped her across the lawn, to her house, before returning home. I'd left the box Bea had brought me on the kitchen table, and as I went to pick it up, I noticed Karma was curled up inside it. I shook my head and carried it and her into my office to try to make heads or tails of the contents.

An hour or so later, I had everything put in some kind of order and put away in my file cabinet. It would have to wait for another day.

The next week seemed to fly by, and I'd done my best to avoid Jason. I just didn't know how I felt, and every time I thought about it, it gave me headache. While I loved my new assignment for the FBI, it involved long, tedious hours. And frankly, I was exhausted.

The file I was currently working on involved a Jane Doe who'd been murdered about fifteen years previously. Her case gave me nightmares, and I woke up screaming and drenched in a cold sweat on more than one occasion.

I'd just gotten back from my run on Sunday morning, when my phone pinged. It was a text from Adrianna, asking me if I wanted to meet for breakfast. I jumped at the chance.

Due to the church crowd, Gil's was packed on Sundays, but we were lucky enough to get a booth by the front window. It was one of my favorite booths in the place because you could see people walking by, and the light streaming through the windows cheered the place up.

We ordered coffee, and chatted about work and what we'd been doing since we last saw each other.

Adrianna leaned across the booth and whispered, "I think the police are watching me."

"What makes you think that?" I said.

"There's been a car parked outside my house the last few nights that I don't recognize. And I think the same car is following me to and from work."

Before I could answer, Tabby came by to refill our coffees and take our breakfast orders.

"Are you sure?" I said.

"About what? That I'm being followed? Yes. That it's the police? No." She sighed.

Now we were getting somewhere.

"Who else could it be?" *Come on, Adrianna, spill your guts.*

She wrapped her hands around her coffee mug and turned to stare out the window.

"I have no idea. An old boyfriend, maybe? I mean, we had a bad breakup."

"Tell me."

"Well, his name was Chad Eastwick. He worked in construction. We met in a bar in Algonac. He was built, you know? Muscular. Nice eyes."

"*Umm-hmm.*" I nodded as I took a bite of my omelet.

"Anyway, we started to date. On our one-year anniversary of going out, he proposed to me, and I said yes." She flashed a brief smile. "He was everything I'd ever wanted. He was possessive of me, and it made me feel safe and loved."

"What happened?"

She sat her fork down on the edge of her plate. "We were so happy. A couple months before the wedding, I wanted to go out with some of my girlfriends. You know, a girl's night out."

I nodded.

"Chad became furious. He accused me cheating on him. He completely lost it. I'd never seen him lose his temper like that before." She frowned, as if she was still trying to figure everything out. "I told him it wasn't true, that I loved him."

I sipped my coffee. "Did that calm him down?"

"No. The opposite, in fact." She dabbed her eyes with a napkin. "He attacked me! Hit me and screamed at me. It was all I could do to get out of there." Her body shuddered at the memory.

"Oh, my God. That's terrible. Did you call the police?"

She hung her head. "No. I chalked it up to a one-time thing, and he apologized the next day."

I reached across the table and gave her hand a small squeeze. "Adrianna, I'm so sorry that happened to you."

"Thank you." She withdrew her hand, "Anyway, things just got worse. Every time I wanted to go out with my friends, or go to my parent's house without him, it would set him off again. I couldn't take it anymore, and broke off the engagement."

"I don't blame you." I wiped my mouth with a napkin.

She nodded. "Then he started stalking me—texting me, sending me flowers, following me everywhere. It was terrible. I've moved around a lot, but he always seems to find me." She gazed out the window.

I could see her scanning the people and cars as they went by.

"Do you think he murdered that poor woman?" I looked at her, expectantly.

She shook her head and shrugged.

"Have you told the police this?"

"No. He would never murder anyone." She gave me a defiant look.

I sat back in the booth. *She still loves him.*

"You have to tell the police what you just told me. If you're so sure he didn't do anything wrong, then there's nothing to worry about. A woman was murdered, Adrianna."

"I know. But it wasn't Chad!" She reached into her purse and pulled out some money for her bill. "I have to go. Let's get together again soon." She got up and moved to my side of the booth, then leaned over and hugged my shoulders. "I'm so glad we're friends."

And she was gone.

I sat back, stunned. *What the hell just happened?*

As I walked home from Gil's, I realized I had a problem.

Do I tell Nate about my conversation with Adrianna?

Chad Eastwick could be the killer, and it still puzzled me as to why she didn't tell the police about him. Not just that, she defended him.

I let myself into the house, locked the door, and set the alarm. Then went back to work on the Jane Doe file I'd been working on for the last few days. Karma followed me and curled up on the soft baby blanket I'd put on the corner of my desk for her.

As hard as I tried to concentrate on the task at hand, my mind kept wandering back to Adrianna and Chad Eastwick.

Realizing all hope of getting any work done was lost, I switched databases, and after a little bit of searching, found a guy I believed to be the right Chad Eastwick. He lived close to Algonac, a town about fifteen miles north of Hope Harbor, and he was about the same age as Adrianna. Another tip-off was that he worked in construction. His criminal record wasn't long, but it was telling. He'd been arrested for aggravated assault a couple years ago.

Hmm. That fit the time frame that Adrianna said they were together.

According to what court records I could access, the case did involve Adrianna, but the charges had been dropped.

He'd had a couple speeding tickets, but that didn't make him a killer. I found him on social media, and spent some time going through it. He appeared to have an interest in true crime. Interesting, but it didn't prove anything. I belonged to several true crime groups online myself.

It appeared that he also liked to write. I went back further in his social media, and came upon some disturbing posts from a year before. He'd posted excerpts from a few short stories he'd written. Dark, disturbing stories that dealt with the horrors of human trafficking, bondage, and torture. Granted, they were just excerpts, and taken out of context, but it was enough to cause a cold chill to run down my spine.

Before closing out the page, I printed a picture of him and put him on my board, under the title, *Suspects.*

As I shut down my computer and went around the house, turning off the lights, I knew I wasn't any closer to solving my real problem—do I go to the police with all this information?

I tossed and turned most the night, and gave up all hopes of sleep at 5:00 a.m. I got up and changed into my running clothes. It was still dark, but I reasoned there were more than enough streetlights on my path for it to be relatively safe.

The run did little to clear my head, but I still stopped in at Gil's to grab a cup of coffee to-go, before walking the rest of the way home. I picked up the house and spent the day working on the project for the FBI. I knew I should start on Bea's files, but I just wasn't in the mood.

As I worked, I kept thinking about Chad Eastwick. Adrianna said they had met at a bar in Algonac.

Hmm. Maybe a night out would do me good.

I shut down my computer and got ready to go out. I called my friend Maddy to see if she wanted to go, but she had a date.

Three bars later, I finally spotted Chad shooting pool at one of the local bars. I perched at a stool at the bar, close—but not too close—to the pool tables, and ordered a diet soda. I made it a rule not to drink and drive—ever.

When they'd finished the game, Chad walked over to the bar and ordered a beer. He glanced my way, and I smiled at him. He paid for his beer and took the stool next to me. We exchanged names and greetings.

"I haven't seen you in here before." He gazed at me with his large green eyes.

"First time." I took a sip of my soda.

We chatted about our jobs. He was still in construction, but now owned his own remodeling company.

As we talked, I couldn't help but notice he seemed like a really nice guy. He asked a lot of questions and actually listened to the answers. In return, when I asked him questions, he answered them completely, not just one- or two-word responses. Impressive.

We spent the evening laughing and dancing. He tried to teach me how to play pool, and it soon became evident that it wasn't my forte. At midnight, I decided to leave, and he walked me to my truck. Such a gentleman. We agreed to get together tomorrow night.

On the way home, I thought about my evening with Chad. I could understand why Adrianna was attracted to him. He had a great sense of humor, was easy to talk to, and paid attention to a girl in a way that made her feel special. But then again, sociopaths had a lot of the same traits.

When I pulled into the driveway, I noticed that Bea was peeking out the curtains of her living room window. I could feel the disproving glare as I got out of my Jeep and let myself into the house.

I tossed my keys and bag on the kitchen table and sighed. Eventually, I was going to have to talk to Bea about her nosiness and keeping tabs on my comings and goings. I loved her dearly, but what I did and when I did it was none of her business.

Even though it was late, I was still wired from being out for the evening, so I fired up my computer to check my email.

Pam Davis, the president of the Hope Harbor Historical Society, had sent a note reminding me of the Polar Plunge and open house tomorrow.

Damn! I'd completely forgotten about it.

I had to attend because I was anxious to find out if they'd received the grant that would allow me to continue my work on the witch cemetery that laid deep in the woods by the old Rockman house.

A few minutes later, I decided to run Chad through another database, and discovered that he was literally off the grid for about six months last year. There wasn't any activity on his credit report, and no postings on social media or anywhere else I could find.

What the hell?

Due to federal and state laws that classify certain records as unavailable without the person's permission, there was little else I could find out that I didn't already know. Maybe Adrianna would have an idea of what happened to him.

I checked court and prison records for not only the county and state, but the federal system as well, and there weren't any. So he hadn't been in jail.

Well, that was a relief.

At 2:00 a.m., I wearily climbed into bed. Tomorrow was going to be a long day, and I had to be sharp for my date with Chad that night.

I managed to crawl out of bed at 6:00 a.m. The morning dawned crisp and cold, with a biting wind blowing in off the lake. I was sluggish, and it felt like I was running through wet cement.

Instead of my usual five miles, all I could muster was a weak three before stopping at Gil's for coffee, and I decided to walk along the boardwalk in the park on my way home. The firemen were busy putting a large hole in the lake by the beach, for the men and women who were brave enough to venture into the water for the plunge. It was, after all, for charity. But to me it wasn't worth freezing to death. However, I would definitely sign a few pledge cards to support the children's hospital.

Around noon, I got bundled up and strolled down to the park. The atmosphere was like that of a carnival. All the people participating in the polar plunge were dressed in colorful costumes. I saw clowns, superheroes, and people in costumes I couldn't even begin to figure out.

Frank Dixon, the owner of Dixon Books, was dressed in a pair of flannel sleepers that resembled a giraffe pattern, with a large inflatable rubber duck innertube around his ample waist. He was struggling to hold his satchel and innertube. I rushed over to help him, all the while trying not to laugh.

"Can you hold my satchel?" He looked sheepish. "It has my keys, wallet, and a change of clothes in it."

"Of course." I took the bag from his hand. "Good luck!" I gave him a kiss on the cheek.

A small contingent from the high school marching band were in full dress uniforms, and filled the cold air with the harmonious sounds of their instruments.

I paused to pledge some money on Frank Dixon's pledge card before getting a cup of hot cocoa from one of the street vendors.

The firemen and the dive team were ready to go, and I walked out onto the pier that jutted into the lake so I would have a good view. The mayor gave a short speech before signaling it was time for the festivities to begin.

The firemen were allowing five people to run into the frigid water at a time, and each time, the crowd would clap and cheer. As soon as the people plunged, the dive team stepped in an helped them out of the water to warmed blankets.

I whooped and cheered for Frank as he entered the water, and his face turned ashen white. He started to collapse, and two divers rushed to his side and carried him out of the water to waiting first responders.

As I started to run down the pier toward Frank, someone rushed over with two warm blankets and covered Frank up. The first responders moved him to a stretcher and wheeled him over to an ambulance.

I fought through the crowd and ran over to where he was.

"Frank! Frank! It's Zoey. Are you okay?" I peered into the back of the ambulance.

"Are you a relative?" said one of the first responders.

"She's the closest thing I have to family." Frank's voice sounded weak. "Please."

Without waiting for permission, I scampered up into the ambulance, knelt by Frank and took his hand. He gave mine a quick squeeze.

He'd been hooked up to oxygen, and they were doing an EKG. One of the responders got into the driver's seat, and we were on our way to the hospital.

Frank closed his eyes, and I noticed that he suddenly looked old. The lines in his face seemed to be deeper, and his hair a little grayer.

I'd known Frank since I was a little girl. Uncle Felix would take me to the bookstore every weekend I was with him, and we would spend what seemed like hours selecting just the right book to add to our collection.

Over the years, Frank and I formed a close friendship, and would spend time talking about different books and authors. He always seemed to know a fun fact about my favorite authors, and I enjoyed spending time with him. Still do. To see him in such a weakened state broke my heart.

We got to the hospital, and Frank was whisked away into an examination room. A triage nurse led me to a chair and started asking me questions about him. Most of them, I couldn't answer. And then I remembered I had his satchel.

I opened the bag and took out his wallet. I felt horrible going through his personal things, but I had to find his insurance card. Once the intake nurse was satisfied, I was left alone with my thoughts.

A half-hour later, an older doctor called for who was with Frank. I stood and went over to him.

"I'm Doctor Briggs. Your dad didn't have a heart attack, but his body suffered quite a shock when he hit that cold water. I'm going to keep him here overnight for observation, but he should be fine."

"Thank you, Doctor. Will he need any special care when he's released?"

"He's going to need bed rest for a couple days, at least. Is that going to be a problem?"

"No."

I hesitated. Frank lived alone, but an idea began to form in my head.

"Not at all," I said.

"You can see him now. He's in exam room three."

"Thanks," I headed there.

When I entered the room, Frank was sitting up in bed, enjoying a container of chocolate pudding.

"Zoey!" He smiled.

"How are you feeling?" I sat in the chair next to his bed.

"Better. Thanks for being there for me. Can you do me a favor? Can you take my keys and go to my apartment to get me some pajamas? I feel like an idiot in these sleepers."

"Of course!" I burst out laughing.

Frank laughed as well.

We spent a few more minutes talking before I called a ride-share service to take me back into town. Using Frank's keys, I let myself into the bookstore and went through the back room to the set of stairs leading to his studio apartment. I packed him some pajamas, clean underwear, and a change of clothes for him to come home in.

I walked home and took my truck back to the hospital to drop off his things. I wanted to stay, but I still had to put in an appearance at the historical society open house, and get ready for my *date* with Chad.

B efore I left to go to the open house, I stopped by Bea's and told her about Frank's situation. She was thrilled to have a house guest for a few days, and immediately set about getting the guest room ready.

By the time I got to the Hope Harbor Historical Society's museum, the open house was in full swing. The rooms were packed with townsfolk, and I worked my way into the dining room to get a hot cup of cider.

Pam Davis, the president of the historical society, caught my eye, and I elbowed through the crowded room, toward her. We exchanged greetings, and I spent a few minutes filling her in on how Frank was doing.

"Have you heard anything about the grant?" I said.

"Yes!" Her eyes sparkled. "We got it. So in the spring, after the snow melts and the weather warms up, we want you to continue your research into the witch cemetery. We'll meet in a month or two to discuss the details."

"Sounds great!"

We chatted for a few more minutes, before she was called away to answer some questions about one of the exhibits. I milled around, chatting with a few more people, before slipping out the front door to get ready to meet Chad.

Given the events of the day, I wasn't in the mood to go out with Chad, but I had to find out more about him. As I drove to the bar, I began to feel guilty for going out with him under such false pretenses.

When I pulled into the bar parking lot, I saw Chad waiting for me out front. We exchanged greetings and settled into a high-top table. Chad ordered our drinks.

"I was so glad to get out of Hope Harbor, with all these horrible things going on. A woman being left on a porch, with her throat cut. Did you hear about it?" I took a sip of wine.

He nodded. "I heard about it. Poor girl."

"The body was left on the porch of a friend of mine."

"Oh, really?" He looked at me. "Who was that?"

"Adrianna Martinelli." I said, as casually as I could muster.

He sat up straight and stared at me. "Karma's a bitch. I feel bad for the woman who died. I really do. But it's about time someone called Adrianna out on her crap."

"Her crap?" I leaned forward, towards him.

The music was loud, and I wanted to make sure I heard every word.

"What do you mean?"

"Adrianna and I were engaged a couple years ago." His eyes took on a faraway look as the memory replayed in his mind. "Things were great. And then she turned into this controlling possessive woman." He shook his head.

"Go on."

"I tried everything I could think of to make her feel secure, but nothing worked. I ended up calling off the engagement. I didn't know what else to do." He held his hands out, palms up.

I nodded. "That must have been hard."

"It was. But then the real hell began. Adrianna was furious. She showed up at my house one night, and I tried to explain everything to her, but she started to rage, and attacked me. It was all I could do to get her out of the house."

"Interesting." I looked him in the eye. "Adrianna tells a completely different story. She told me that you assaulted her, and then you stalked her!"

His face turned red, and a vein on his neck swelled under his skin.

"I never!" he said, through gritted teeth. "What kind of guy do you think I am?"

"I don't know." I decided to push a button or two and see what happened. "What kind of guy are you? I saw your posts on social media, and they were filled with stories of torture and bondage. Sounds like you're a sick, sadistic kind of guy."

In one swift movement, he was out of his chair and standing next to me. He grabbed my upper arm and yanked me out of the stool so hard I almost fell over. He steadied me and handed me my bag. Then he walked me outside, never letting up on his claw-like grip on my arm.

When we got to the parking lot, he turned me around to face him, and put both his hands on my shoulders.

"Listen. I don't know why you're helping Adrianna turn my life back into a living hell, but that little bitch deserves everything that happens to her." He took one of his hands off my shoulder and grabbed a handful of hair on the back of my head.

He pulled my face within inches of his.

"Let me go!" I screamed, and glanced around the parking lot for help, but the lot was void of people.

I squirmed in an attempt to get away, but he just tightened his grip.

"It would be in your own best interest to get in your car and go back to where you came from." He sneered and jerked my head backwards before he released me and stomped back toward the bar.

My knees buckled, and I collapsed on the gravel-covered ground of the parking lot. My body was trembling, and I put my hands to my face and started to sob. It took me a minute to collect myself. Then I got up and picked up my bag before stumbling to my Jeep. I let myself in and locked the door. I sat there for a minute or two, gathering my thoughts. I'd definitely pushed the right buttons, and in my mind, he was totally capable of murder.

After pulling out of the parking lot, toward home, I called Nate and asked him to meet me at my house.

"Are you okay?" he said.

My voice must have still been shaky.

"No. No, I'm not. See you in a few minutes." I hung up before he could say anything else.

I wanted time to calm down before I talked to him.

He was waiting on my porch when I pulled into the driveway. I pulled my keys out of my bag and let us in. He followed me into the kitchen, and we sat on the stools at the island.

"Tell me what happened." His words were as smooth as a fine whiskey, his voice calm and gentle.

I took a deep breath and spilled my guts. I told him about my conversation with Adrianna, and his hands clenched into fists when I told him about my confrontation with Chad Eastwick.

Before he could say anything after I'd finished, someone was pounding on my front door. Nate motioned for me to stay put, and stalked toward the front door. It was then that I noticed the gun in the holster on his belt. He rested his hand on the butt of the weapon, and slid his index finger down to release the safety.

When he opened the door, Jason burst inside, brushed past Nate and rushed to my side.

"Are you okay?

Nate pulled up like a bat out of hell.

"What happened?"

Nate joined us in the kitchen and filled him in on my eventful evening. As he talked, I watched Jason's face. His puzzled expression turned to anger.

"What the hell were you thinking?" Jason yelled at me.

"I…I…"

Truth be told, I didn't have a good reason. It'd been a stupid idea all the way around.

Nate maneuvered between Jason and I.

"Shut it down, Jason. The last thing she needs right now is to be abused by another man." Nate glared at Jason.

"You're right." Jason relaxed his shoulders. "I was just so scared." He sidestepped Nate and took my hand. "Come here."

I got down off the stool, and he enveloped me in a hug. His strong arms around me made me feel safe. We held onto each other for a brief time, before I released from his grasp and got back on my chair.

"I'm going to bring Chad Eastwick in for questioning." Nate looked at me. "Do you want to press charges?"

I shook my head. "No, it's okay. I'm fine. The entire situation was my fault."

What the hell? Now I was defending him.

Nate gave Jason a curt nod before leaving out the front door. Jason sat on a stool next to mine.

"Zoey, I understand you have this insatiable curiosity. But tonight, it could have gotten you hurt. Or worse. Do you understand?"

I nodded.

"You have to stop investigating things that are none of your business. In case you've forgotten, you're not a cop, or a private investigator, and you have no formal training. Why can't you just be normal? You know, like other women."

"And what do normal women do?" I could feel my blood start to boil.

"You know." He sat back in his seat. "They go to work, go out with friends, take care of their families. What they don't do is go off half-cocked, and bait a possible murderer."

Well, he had a point there.

"You're right." I got off my stool and headed toward the front door.

He followed me.

"They don't go off half-cocked, after a possible murderer." I opened the door for him, and he walked onto the porch. "Next time, I'll have a better plan." I slammed the door in his face.

"Zoey!" he yelled, through the locked door.

"Good night, Jason!" I set the alarm, then peered through the front blinds and saw him walk back across the street, to his house. "*Ugh!* Men."

I poured a glass of wine and disappeared into my office. After booting up my computer, I typed out everything I could remember about my confrontation with Chad.

Good thing Adrianna got away from him. No wonder she moved around so much—he was an extremely dangerous man.

I shut my computer down and got changed into my pajamas. There were red marks on my arms from where Chad had grabbed me, and I was pretty sure that by morning I would be sporting some nice bruises.

Karma and I got into bed, and she curled up alongside me, sensing that I needed her comfort tonight. As I laid there and stroked her soft fur, I thought about what Jason had said.

Before falling asleep, I decided that he and I needed to have a serious discussion. Jason had said he loved me, and I knew he meant it. But was he in love with the person I am, or the person he wanted me to be?

The next morning, I got ready to go pick up Frank from the hospital.

When I walked into his room, he was sitting up in bed, eating an unappetizing-looking breakfast. He gave me a broad smile when he saw me, and I was relieved to see his color had returned.

I explained my plan for him to stay with Bea while I ran the bookstore until he was back on his feet.

"Oh, yes, I know Bea. She goes to my church. I'm sorry to be such a bother."

I put my hand on his shoulder. "You're no trouble at all. I think Bea's kind of looking forward to it, and I know I'm going to enjoy running the store for a few days. Is there anything I need to know?"

Frank spent a few minutes explaining how to get into the store's email and other necessary programs.

"I really appreciate this, Zoey."

Before I could answer, the doctor came into the room, and once we explained our plan for Frank, he signed the discharge papers.

I went out and pulled my Jeep up to the doors while Frank was getting dressed. A few minutes later, an orderly wheeled him out. On the way to Bea's, we stopped by his apartment over the bookstore and picked up clothing and personal items he would need while he was staying with her.

As soon we pulled into Bea's driveway, she came outside to help Frank—amid his protests—into the house. I carried in his bag and put it in the guest room. When I returned to the living room, Frank was settled on the couch with a blanket over his legs, and Bea was fussing in the kitchen to make him *something decent to eat.*

Smiling to myself, I said my goodbyes and went home. I had some things to get ready before I opened the bookstore.

I packed up my laptop and a couple of the files I was working on, and changed into a nice pair of pants and a sweater. I wanted to be presentable to the customers. Then I put Karma in her carrier and packed her travel bowls, some food, and a disposable litter box I'd picked up at the store. Every bookstore needs a cat, I reasoned.

The familiar peal of the bell on the front door greeted me as I entered the shop. I stopped and took a deep breath. The smell of a used bookstore is like catnip to people who love books. Woodsy, earthy, and a little musty, all mixed with old leather and aging paper. Intoxicating.

I turned on the lights and sat everything down on the checkout counter before letting Karma out of her carrier to explore. I set up her food and litter box in Frank's office at the back of the store, and showed her where it was.

The bookstore is housed in a building that was erected after the Great Fire of 1870 all but destroyed the city. Mr. Rockman, a wealthy businessman at the time, gave no-interest or low-interest loans to the business owners in town to rebuild. And rebuild they did.

At the front of the store, two large bay windows jutted out from the front of the building on either side of the old wooden door. Bookshelves snaked around the store's perimeter, stopping only to allow for the checkout counter to sit in the center of one of the side walls.

Other bookshelves were installed in rows throughout the store, and arranged in such a way that you could see down almost all the rows from the cash register. Disbursed in little nooks throughout the store were comfy overstuff chairs. Sconces hung on the walls by the chairs to allow a patron to linger and have adequate reading light.

An inspection of the small lights indicated it'd been a long time since the glass shades had been cleaned, so I took all the shades off, washed and dried them, and put them back.

While I was doing that, Karma was getting used to her new surroundings, and was cautiously exploring this strange but wonderful place.

I'd just finished checking the email for the store when the first customers arrived. I let them browse, and heard them fuss over Karma, who soaked up all the attention she could get.

Pam Davis from the historical society came in, and we exchanged greetings. I followed her back to the history section.

"Looking for anything special?" I said.

"Actually, I was looking for a book on cemetery restoration." She tilted her head sideways so she could read the titles. "When you get finished with your research on the witch cemetery, I think we're going to make it a project to restore it."

"That's a fabulous idea! I'll be more than happy to help."

She straightened her lanky body and put her hand on my arm. "You're such a dear."

I went back to counter and did a quick search on my computer. "Here's one," I called back to her. "I'll order it in for you."

Pam joined me at the counter. "Perfect. Thanks, Zoey." She headed for the door.

There was a steady stream of traffic through the store until after lunch. Running a bookstore was more difficult than I anticipated, but I was loving every minute of it.

When it quieted down, I pulled out my laptop and started to work on one of the files for the FBI. I was getting closer to finding the identity of a Jane Doe, and was getting excited about being able to bring closure to a family, regarding the fate of their loved one.

Just as I made one more connection, I heard the bell on the front door. I glanced up and saw Rodger Frost and another man enter the store.

"Professor Frost. So nice to see you again."

He looked at me, and I could tell it took a minute or two for it to register where he knew me from.

"Oh, Miss…ah, yes. You were at my lecture at the college, with Miss Perkins, yes?"

"Exactly. I'm Zoey Callaway. Is there something I can help you find?"

"Yes! Miss Callaway, of course. Where's Frank?" Rodger looked around the store.

"He's out for a couple days."

I didn't think Frank's health was anyone's business.

"Ahh. He was holding a book for me," Rodger said, disappointment registering on his face.

"Yes, I saw it this morning. I'll be right back." I headed back to Frank's office.

I'd remembered seeing a book wrapped in a piece of notebook paper with Rodger's name on it.

I retrieved the book and returned to the cash register. Rodger and his companion were browsing the shelves. When Rodger turned around to go down another aisle, I noticed Karma was curled up in his arms, and he was stroking her back.

A few minutes later, he came up to the cash register, with Karma still in his grip. His companion put three books—all biographies—on the counter. Only when Rodger had to pull out his wallet did he set Karma down.

"About time Frank got a cat in here." He handed me his credit card.

"Actually, this is Karma. She's my cat." I ran his card through the machine.

As I wrapped up his books, we chatted about the cat, and whether I'd started in on Bea's genealogy

"I hope to get started on it next week," I said. "I've just been so busy."

"I'm at your disposal should you have questions." He bowed slightly.

"Thank you. I may just take you up on that."

He picked up his bag and extended his hand toward me.

"Nice to see you again, Miss Callaway."

"You, too, Professor." I shook his hand.

He patted Karma a couple more times before exiting the store with his friend. Just as they were leaving, Nate walked in. While he was wearing jeans and a sweatshirt that matched his bright blue eyes, he had his gun and badge attached to his belt, which gave him an official appearance.

"Hey, I stopped by your house, and Bea yelled out that you were here. What's going on?"

I filled him in on Frank and running the store for a few days.

"What's up with you?" I said.

He reached out to pet Karma, who'd leapt onto the counter.

"I just wanted to see if you were okay after last night."

I rolled up my sleeves and showed him the bruises that'd been left by Chad's grip.

"Other than that, I'm fine. Did you question Chad?"

"Yeah, we brought him in last night. He has an alibi for the murder, but it's a weak one. I also had a talk with him about how he'd treated you. He seemed to be remorseful." Nate shook his head.

"Any other leads on Sienna's death?"

"Not really." He sighed. "We searched her apartment and went through her computer. Nothing really there. She belonged to a couple online dating sites. But nowadays, who doesn't?"

"I don't."

"You don't have to join a dating site. You have Jason, remember?" A wry grin spread across his face.

"Who had she been talking to?"

"A few guys. We've talked to most of them, but she didn't even go out with any of them. It's a dead end."

"*Hmm.* What about her cell phone?"

"We haven't found it, or the primary crime scene. Frankly, we're stumped." He folded his arms and rested them on the counter.

I reached put my hand on his forearm. "I'm sorry. I'm sure something will come up."

"Thanks." He put his hand over mine. "You've spent a lot of time with Adrianna. What do you think of her?"

I withdrew my hand and folded my arms across my chest.

"That's hard to answer. On one hand, I feel sorry for her. But on the other, there's just something off about her, but I can't put my finger on it."

As we talked, I filled him in on what I'd found out during my background check of Adrianna—her frequent moves and job changes the past couple years.

Nate listened intently. "So you think Chad's been stalking her since they broke up?"

"I can't say." I shrugged. "To hear her tell it, yes. But—"

"But you're not sure if you believe her."

I shook my head. "It's not a question of belief. Her behavior alone says that she's afraid of something. I'm just not sure it's Chad. Although, he sure acts the part."

We stood staring at each other, letting all the possibilities play out in our heads.

I glanced at the clock. "I've got to lock up the store."

"I'll help you, and follow you home. Bea invited me for dinner. I'm pretty sure she's going to ask you, too."

"Good!" I smiled. "I'm starving."

Nate and I corralled Karma back into her carrier, and after taking care of a few more things, I turned off the lights and locked up the store.

When I pulled in the driveway, Bea yelled out her door to come over for dinner.

"Be there in a minute!" I unloaded Karma from my Jeep.

I put her in the house and gave her dinner before heading across the front yard, to Bea's house. When I walked in, Nate and Frank were sitting in the living room, engaged in a conversation about the NHL playoffs, and Bea was bustling around the kitchen.

Atlas, Bea's German Shepherd, greeted me, and I spent a minute fawning over him before helping Bea get dinner on the table.

The conversation over dinner was lively and filled with laughter. Frank shared some of the more amusing stories about running his bookstore for the last twenty years, and had us in stitches.

During dinner, I couldn't help but notice the adoring looks Bea was giving Frank, and how she fussed over him. While that would annoy me to no end, Frank seemed to enjoy the attention.

After dinner, Frank and Nate retired to the living room to watch the hockey game, while I helped Bea put away the food and clean the kitchen.

"It's so nice to have a man around again." Bea rinsed off a plate.

"I'm sure it is. He looks good." I glanced into the living room.

Bea looked at Frank. "He does look better, but he's still a lot weaker than he's letting on. I'll be right back."

She went into the living room and grabbed a throw blanket off the back of the couch to cover Frank's legs with it. He thanked her and patted her hand.

While she was taking care of Frank, I finished loading the dishwasher. Bea fed Atlas, and after he ate, he went into the living room and curled up at Frank's feet.

We joined Frank and Nate in the living room, but I doubt they even knew we were there they were so engrossed in the game.

When the first period ended, I noticed Frank was dosing off in the chair. I caught Nate's gaze and nodded toward Frank. Nate got up from the couch, and I got out of my chair.

After thanking Bea for dinner and saying goodbye to Frank, Nate walked me home.

I fell into bed, exhausted, but looking forward to another day at the bookstore. Karma must have been tired, too, because she fell asleep next to me before giving herself a good cleaning.

8

I got to the bookstore early. I wanted to redo the displays in the windows at the front of the store. After turning Karma loose, I removed all the books and other items from the windows. I didn't know how long they'd been in there, but they were covered in dust and cobwebs that made me sneeze as I cleaned and re-shelved them.

Since it was mid-March, I decided that spring displays would work best and maybe be a good omen for a break in the weather. It'd been unusually cold and snowy for this time of year, and me, along with most of the townspeople, were so over winter it wasn't even funny.

I browsed through the store with a book cart, and selected some books from the children's department that had bunnies, baby chicks, and other cute little animals that weren't overly Easter, but had bright spring-like covers. In the other sections of the store, I picked out spring gardening and landscaping books. I also added some romance and cozy mysteries to the mix.

When I got back to the front, I realized I needed props. So I scrounged around the storage room and found a few items that would work.

I finished the windows just before the store was due to open, but took a few minutes to walk outside to admire my handywork. As I stood on the sidewalk in front of the bookstore, I saw police cars, a fire truck, and an ambulance come racing down Main Street, with lights and sirens on. They were heading to the park!

As much as I wanted to go see what was going on, I knew I couldn't leave the store.

Damn it!

I peered down the street, trying to catch a glimpse of what was going on, but I couldn't see anything except that the first responders were down close to the beach.

I'd forgotten to put on my jacket before going outside, and I wrapped my T-shirt around my shivering body as I craned my neck for a view of the activity.

The cold weather won. I gave up trying to see what was going on, and went back into the store. I stopped to crank the heat up a couple of degrees, before changing the sign on the front door from *closed* to *open*. A couple customers came in and asked what was going on at the park, and I had to tell them I didn't know.

The cash register rested on a wood-topped display cabinet, and housed the more valuable books in the store. As the customers browsed and fawned over Karma, I took the books out of the case and washed the glass. I cleaned the books like Frank had taught me to years ago, before replacing them in the display case. The dust jackets really should be wrapped in acid-free archival covers, but I couldn't find any in the store, the storage room, or Frank's office. I made a note to myself to order some.

The morning hours ticked away slowly, as there were few customers, and I was so curious about what happened at the park this morning it was eating me alive. I tried to kill time by getting some work done on the Jane Doe case, but I couldn't concentrate.

I ended up playing on the Internet, and was shocked to discover that Frank didn't have a website for the store, or try to sell any of the books online. What the hell? I'd have to have a talk with him about that.

Around noon, I heard the bell on the front door ring, and glanced up to see Nate walk into the store with a bag from Gil's.

"Thought you could use some lunch." He put the bag on the counter next to the register.

"Thanks!" I reached into the bag and pulled out a carry-out box. "Is this mine?"

He nodded.

"What happened at the park this morning?" I opened the box to find a hamburger and fries.

A grim look clouded his face. "A jogger found the body of a dead woman by the pier. She was propped up against one of the park light poles."

It took a minute for what he'd said to register.

"What? I ran along the pier at about five, and there wasn't anything there. I would have seen it, right?"

"More than likely." He shrugged. "There's more."

I took a bite of my burger and looked at him expectantly.

"There was a note, like before, addressed to Adrianna." He put the rest of his burger back into the carry-out box.

"What did it say?"

"I can't tell you. We're holding it back, even from the press. Plus, Jason would kill me if he knew I'd told you this much."

"Jason doesn't control me or my life." I got up from my stool.

Enough was enough. What the hell was going on?

Nate stood and put his carry-out box in the garbage.

"I have to go. Sorry, Zoey. But if Adrianna confides in you about what the note said, there's no way I can stop that, now is there?" He winked before disappearing out the front door.

I smiled at his not-so-subtle hint as I cleaned up the counter after I'd finished my lunch.

Wondering how Adrianna was holding up, I texted her and told her I'd heard what happened, and asked if she was okay. She texted back that she was just leaving for work when the detective had shown up, and that she was a mess. She told me to come over.

I wished I could. I told her I was at the bookstore and why, but promised to come over after it closed.

Just as I put my phone back into my bag, Jason came in at the same time a couple of customers entered.

"Hey." He walked up to the counter. "Did you hear what happened?"

"Yeah. A couple people were talking about it when they came into the store."

He opened his mouth to say something, but Mitzi Davis, one of the elders who lived in town, approached the counter.

"Hi, Mitzi," I said. "Did you need something?"

She asked about Frank, and I explained the situation to her.

"I see." She put a finger on her chin. "Do you know if he has an Easter or spring crochet book?"

I moved out from behind the counter and put my arm around her slumped shoulders.

"Let's go see."

We inched back to the craft section of the store. Mitzi had horrible osteoporosis, and it'd caused her spine to curve. It took her a little longer to get somewhere, but bless her heart, she still got out and about when the weather permitted.

I settled her in one of the chairs and searched the crochet books until I found a few that could pass for having spring patterns. I handed them to her as I found them so she could look through them.

As she browsed through the pages, Karma ventured over and jumped up on the arm of her chair.

"Oh, precious." A broad smile crossed Mitzi's face as she reached out to pet Karma.

Crochet forgotten, she cooed and whispered to Karma, and told me the story of her cat, Munchie, that she'd just had to put down.

A tear rolled down her cheek. "I miss him so."

I put my hand on hers. "I'm so sorry, Mitzi."

I don't know how long I sat cross-legged on the floor in front of Mitzi while she cuddled Karma, but I didn't care. The comfort my cat brought to her in those moments were worth the time.

Finally, she turned her attention back to the crochet books.

"I'll take them all."

I got up and gathered the books for her. I put Karma on the floor and helped Mitzi out of the chair and back to the register. It was past closing time, but I didn't want to rush her.

I wrapped the books in tissue paper and put them in a bag. Jason helped her out of the store, and she tottered down the sidewalk, toward home.

"I'm sorry, Jason." I turned off the store lights. "I'd really like to talk, but I have plans."

His jaw locked. "With who?"

"A friend."

I locked up the store and took Karma to my Jeep. Without another word to Jason, I dropped Karma off at home, and when she was happily munching on dinner, I left and drove the few short blocks to Adrianna's.

When I pulled into her driveway, the house was dark and her car was gone.

What the hell?

I knocked on the door and rang the doorbell.

Nothing.

I pulled my cell phone out of my bag and texted her.

She texted back, saying she was sorry, but had gone to spend the night with a friend. That she was too scared to stay by herself, and asked me to meet up with her tomorrow for breakfast.

Damn it!

I drove back into town and stopped by Gil's to get something to eat. The smell of burgers and fries greeted me when I walked through the door. My stomach growled in response. I was starving.

A group of older men were sitting at one of the large tables, and seemed to be engrossed in a conversation. I slid into a booth close to them.

One of the things I learned from hanging out in Hope Harbor with Uncle Felix for a number of years was that men tend to gossip more than women, and their gossip is much more interesting.

Dan Thomas, who had his back to me, was doing most the talking. I leaned forward so I could eavesdrop.

"Yeah. Poor Ben. He was really shaken up."

I knew Ben was his son, and a little older than me. I'd seen him running a few times along the pier.

"I bet." One of the men shook his head.

"He said it was gruesome," Dan said. "But the worst part was the note. I told you he said it was safety-pinned to the poor girl's neck, right?"

Dan was milking his fifteen minutes of fame for everything it was worth. I wanted to scream at him to get to the point.

"Ben said it was the weirdest thing." Dan shook his head. "The note had the initials, A.M., and then the words, *You can't hide from your past.*

So that's what it said! So much for Nate wanting to keep the contents of the note quiet. It was obvious that the A.M. was Adrianna Martinelli. But why didn't the killer spell out her name, like last time?

Tabby came by the table to drop off my diet soda, and I ordered a tuna salad sandwich and fries. By the time she'd left my table, the men had moved on to speculating who A.M. could be, and worrying about whether there was a serial killer on the loose in Hope Harbor.

They had a valid concern, and it made me angry with Adrianna. I knew she was holding something back from me and the police. Why wouldn't she tell them what was going on so maybe all this madness would stop?

I flagged Tabby down and ordered a hot fudge brownie and ice cream for dessert. It was my favorite. I hardly ever ate one, because of the calories. But tonight I was frustrated, and I wanted—no, I needed—the sweet treat.

After savoring every bite, I paid my bill and drove home. As I got out of my truck, Bea stuck her head out her front door and yelled at me to come over. I sprinted across the lawn and said hi to Frank, who was sitting in the recliner in the living room, sipping a cup of hot cocoa.

"I've been hearing good things about you," Frank said, a huge smile on his face. "They love the cat."

"Thanks, Frank. It's been fun." I sat on the couch.

"I went to the doctor today, and I'm fit as a fiddle. You are officially off bookstore duty. I'll open the store tomorrow."

"That's great!" I showed more enthusiasm than I felt.

I'd loved spending all day at the store.

I slipped the store key off my key ring and gave it to Frank, then glanced up at Bea, who was making herself busy in the kitchen, and saw a look of sadness on her face. Some people just aren't meant to be alone, and it was clear Bea was one of them.

We talked a few more minutes about what had transpired at the store, before I said good night and headed home. I changed into comfy pajamas and curled up on the couch with a blanket to watch the news. I wanted to see what they said about the young woman who'd been dumped in the park.

There wasn't much I didn't already know. The woman, Natalie Zakowski, was from Pershing Woods, a city about forty miles west of Hope Harbor. I made a note of her name, and turned off the television.

I was just about to head into my office to see what I could find out about the murder victim, when the doorbell rang. Thinking maybe it was Bea or Jason, I swung the door open.

Chad Eastwick was standing on my porch.

"CHAD!" I TOOK a step backward.

Adrenaline raced through my body, making me light-headed.

"Hi, Zoey. Can I talk to you, please?"

I was hesitant to let him in the house, but it was cold outside, and I had nosy neighbors.

I stepped aside to let him enter. He entered and shook off the cold. I shut the door, but left it unlocked in case I had to get out of there fast.

I turned to face him and crossed my arms across my chest.

"What do you want, Chad?"

"I came to apologize for the other night. I was way out of line." The sheepish look on his face told me he was telling the truth.

"You attacked me, Chad. I get that Adrianna is a touchy subject for you, but if you keep losing your temper every time her name is mentioned, you're going to end up in jail. Or worse."

"I get that, and I truly am sorry."

"Accepted. Just please get some help for your temper." I felt myself starting to relax.

"'The police hauled me in for questioning about the murders of those women. I didn't do it, Zoey. I'd never do anything like that.'"

It bothered me that he wouldn't look me in the eye when he talked to me, but he could just be feeling bad about the other night.

Wasn't sure I wanted to give him the benefit of the doubt, though.

I opened the front door, indicating our conversation was over. He looked at me and said goodbye, then left. I locked the door behind him and set the alarm.

What the hell was that about? It doesn't do him any good to apologize. Could he be setting up an alibi? Maybe he's trying to get me on his side, and then use me for some terrible reason.

The conversation with Chad left me drained, and I shut off all the lights and went to bed.

The next morning, I felt a little lost since I didn't have to go to the bookstore, so I walked to Gil's to get a coffee to-go, then headed down to the park. I wanted to see where they'd found the body for myself.

It wasn't hard to find. Some of the snow around one of the streetlight poles was stained red, so I determined this was where the woman had been found.

I stood and looked toward Main Street. It puzzled me that he'd picked that spot, because it was at the bottom of the hill. If you were walking along the sidewalk at the north end of the park, you wouldn't have any trouble spotting a body, unless...

I looked up at the light and saw that the bulb had been broken. Of course! I shook my head. He would have to drop the body in cover of darkness, or he ran the risk of being spotted. But there were other parts of the park that were extremely dark, even with the night lights on. What was so special about this spot?

Since most of the blood was in the snow at the rear of the streetlight, it was more than likely that he'd sat her down facing the lake.

I sighed, and after fighting off my gag reflex, sat in the spot she'd been sitting in.

If my calculations were correct, he'd put her facing the pier and the lake. Why not just dump her by Adrianna's house instead almost a mile away? Did he want everyone to know something about Adrianna?

No, that couldn't be right. He had just used her initials on the note.

"What are you doing?"

Jason's voice pierced my thoughts, and I jumped. I'd been so deep down the rabbit hole, I hadn't even heard him come up behind me.

"Trying to figure out why the killer dumped the body here instead of closer to Adrianna's house." I started to get to get up.

He offered me his hand and pulled me to my feet. His handsome features clouded over, and he set his jaw.

"Seriously, Zoey?"

"Seriously. And why did he use her initials, and not write out her name like he did before?" I looked at him.

He shook his head. "I don't know, and it's not up to you to figure it out."

Now I had a choice—do I pick a fight or not.

"True," I said.

"Want breakfast?" His features brightened.

He thought he'd won.

We walked back to Gil's and ordered breakfast. While we were drinking our coffee, I told him about my last two days at the bookstore.

"Sounds like you had fun," he said. "Maybe you should get a real job."

I slammed my knife down on my plate.

"Now you sound like my alcoholic mother. I have a real job."

He glanced up at me. "I'm just saying that maybe if you got out in the real world a little more, you'd be more fulfilled, and not have to look into every murder that occurs in a twenty-mile radius."

"What makes you think I'm not fulfilled?"

He was treading on dangerous ground.

"Bad choice of words. Never mind. So do you think Mitzi Davis is going to be okay?"

I paused, my fork in mid-air. "I don't know. She must be so lonely. Her kids live out of state, and her husband died a few years ago. Now she's lost Munchie. I really should put in more effort to visit her."

His face lit up with a bright smile.

"See, that's the kind of thing most women would do. You've got it."

As much as I wanted to throw a fit and scream at him, I didn't want to cause a scene in the middle of the restaurant during the morning rush.

I drained my coffee cup and gathered up my bag and coat.

"I should go. I don't think we should see each other anymore."

I walked out of the restaurant and started to walk home. My body was shaking, and it wasn't from the cold. He was so traditional in his beliefs. What did he expect? A woman to cook, clean, and be barefoot and pregnant? Well, he was barking up the wrong tree. He didn't even try to follow me, which told me all I needed to know.

When I got home, I didn't even go into the house. I got in my Jeep and headed out to do a little shopping. Nothing calms me more than retail therapy. Everything else would have to wait. Besides, it was Saturday, and a day off wouldn't hurt.

All the major shopping sat a few miles out of town. Various big-box stores, hardware stores, restaurants, and service stores were all crammed into four corners at 23 Mile Road and Gratiot.

I needed cat food and kitty litter, so I pulled into the pet store parking lot. When I walked in, I saw they had an adoption event. Great. Just what I needed. Another animal.

Then I got hit with a great idea. I went over to where they had the cats. There were adorable kittens and older cats in crates.

Frank was standing next to one of the cages.

"What are you doing here?" I said, after we'd exchanged greetings.

"I surrender. I'm going to get a cat for the bookstore." He stuck his finger into one of the cages to play with the kittens. "When I opened the store this morning, six people brought in treats and toys for your cat. So I decided a cat may be good for business."

"Frank." I took his arm to lead him to the adult cats. "You may want an older cat. A kitten is very active and might damage some of the books. Besides, everyone wants kittens, and the older cats have a harder time getting adopted."

"Good point." He peered into a cage that held a handsome tabby.

The cat got up and leaned against the front of the cage so Frank could pet him. Frank signaled to one of the people who were running the event.

"I'll take this one."

Frank walked away with the woman to fill out the adoption application, and I browsed through the rest of the cats. In one of the cages lay a beautiful black cat.

"Hi, kitty,"

The cat, who was laying at the back of the cage, looked at me. All the sadness of the world showed in her eyes.

I called one of the workers over. "What's up with this cat?"

"She's had a hard life," said the young woman. "She's been badly abused. She's healthy now, but we would prefer she went to a single cat house. She needs a lot of love and attention."

"I'll take her. I know the perfect home for her." I told the young woman about Mitzi Davis.

"She sounds perfect! That's exactly what this cat needs." The woman smiled. "I'll get you an application."

Once Frank and I filled out our applications, we shopped for cat supplies. Frank hadn't had a cat in years, and needed everything. I picked up Karma's supplies and then added bowls, toys, a carrier, litter box supplies, and a lot of cat food to my cart, for Mitzi. I crossed my fingers, hoping my plan didn't backfire, and I end up with another cat.

An hour later, Frank and I left the store with our cats and all the supplies. I loaded everything into my Jeep and drove to Mitzi's house. She lived a couple blocks from me, in a two-bedroom ranch, and I saw her peek through the front curtains when I pulled into the driveway.

I unloaded the cat, and by the time I walked up the sidewalk, she had the front door open.

"I brought you someone." I lifted the carrier so she would see the cat.

"Oh, my!" Her face lit up. "Get it out of the cold! It's going to catch its death of dampness."

I sat the carrier on the floor and opened the latch. The fragile cat slowly started to emerge. While we waited, I told Mitzi what the woman had told me about the cat.

When the cat came fully out of its carrier, it went over to Mitzi and looked up at her.

A match made in heaven.

She reached down and patted the cat. While they were getting acquainted, I ran back out to my truck and unloaded the cat supplies. Perhaps I overbought, as it took me three trips to bring everything in.

By the time I'd finished setting up the litter box and putting the other supplies on the kitchen counter, Mitzi and her new cat were sitting on the couch, snuggling. Mitzi had put a blanket over the cat's body to keep her warm. I could hear the purring from the front door.

"I don't know how I'll ever be able to thank you." This time, her eyes were filled with happy tears.

"Seeing you so happy is all the thanks I need." I sat on the couch.

Mitzi was so engrossed in her new pet, I'm pretty sure she didn't even realize I was still there, so I got up and slipped out the front door.

On the way home, I stopped by to see how Frank was doing with his new addition. When I entered the store, a few customers were standing by the checkout, fawning over the new cat. The cat was in kitty heaven, soaking up all the adoration.

Frank stood back and smiled at me. He came out from behind the counter and over to where I was standing.

"I decided to name him Holmes."

"That's perfect."

"Thanks, Zoey. I have to admit, it's going to be nice to have some company at night."

I nodded.

"Do you think he'll be okay when I go out tonight? I'm taking Bea out to a nice dinner to thank her for having me." He blushed.

"I think Holmes will be fine. So you kind of like Bea, huh?" I nudged him with my elbow.

"She's a good woman."

"She is. You better snatch her up before someone else does." I giggled.

Before he could respond, I bounded to the front door and disappeared onto the sidewalk. When I pulled into the driveway, I saw Nate sitting in his pickup, in front of my house.

Now what?

got out of my truck and opened the back liftgate to unload Karma's food and kitty litter. Nate trotted down the porch steps and helped.

"Thanks!" *What does he want?*

He sat the cat food down on the kitchen island. "You okay?"

"Fine. Why wouldn't I be?" I started to put Karma's food away in the cupboard.

"Jason told me you broke up with him." He settled on a stool at the island.

"If you could call it that." I shrugged. "I don't think we were ever really a couple, but whatever." *So that's why he's here.*

He nodded.

"So why do you think the killer used Adrianna's initials on the letter," I said, "and not her full name, like the first one?"

I had my back to him as I was putting things away, but heard him chuckle.

Before he could answer, I said, "And why did he put the body facing the water? And why in that particular spot?"

"Well, those are the million-dollar questions, aren't they? Did you talk to Adrianna?"

"No." I shook my head.

I opened the refrigerator and took out a beer. Held one up, and he nodded.

I glanced out the front window and saw Jason stop in front of my house and stare into the living room.

I shook my head. Talk about stalking.

"I overheard a conversation at Gil's." I fished in a drawer for the bottle opener.

Nate took the bottles out of my hand and twisted off the tops. I felt myself blush.

"It seems that he's choosing his victims at random, because his main target is Adrianna. Although, I don't think that's registered with her yet." I bent down and rested my forearms on the island. "Did you talk to her about that?"

"I've tried to, several times." He shook his head. "She either isn't getting it, or doesn't want to believe it. I've stepped up patrols by her house."

"That's all you can do. I'll talk to her."

Nate stood and drained his beer, then put the empty bottle in the kitchen sink. I followed him to the front door.

"Hey, do you want to go out to dinner tonight?" he said.

"Like a date or something?"

"Or something. Pick you up at seven." He left out the front door.

"Now what the hell does that mean?" I said to Karma, as I locked the door.

She looked at me and meowed.

I glanced at the clock. Still early afternoon. I decided it was time to start on Bea's genealogy. She'd been so patient, and I felt horrible that I hadn't started on it sooner.

Karma curled up on her blanket at the corner of my desk, and I pulled Bea's information out of my file cabinet. I signed into the genealogy website I used, and started entering all the information I had, confirming the dates as I went, if possible.

It was a slow process, but soon a picture was emerging. The website I use gives hints as it makes connections between documents and other people's family trees. I decided to just let the website work for a while, and go back to the Jane Doe case I'd been working on for the FBI.

I couldn't concentrate, so I put the file away and wheeled my murder board into the center of the room. I hadn't updated it in a while, so I found a picture of the latest victim and put it on the board. Then I started writing down what I knew, on index cards, and adding them to the mix. I also added a piece of paper with a big question mark under the suspect heading. I knew Adrianna was still hiding something, and *that something* was probably the key to this whole mess.

Not that Chad wasn't still in the mix. His quick temper and obvious hatred for Adrianna made him a prime suspect. The question was, *Did he have the brains to pull off something like this?*

My mind went back to the note left on the body found on Adrianna's porch. Was it handwritten, or printed out on a computer?

I grabbed my cell phone and called Nate. He told me that both notes were on good card stock, but the words themselves had been printed, not handwritten. I added that information to my board and sighed. That information would certainly broaden the suspect pool. Now all I needed was more suspects.

When I'd finished, I leaned against the edge of my desk and studied the board. I definitely needed to have another talk with Adrianna. A serious one.

By the time I'd finished, it was 5:30, and I had to get ready to go out with Nate. As much as I hated to admit it, I was nervous, but excited. With Jason, it never seemed like we were dating. We'd see each other while we were coming and going because he lived across the street, but he'd never formally asked me out. Just a, *Hey, I'm going to get something to eat. Wanna come?* kind of thing.

It took me forever to figure out what to wear.

You can never go wrong with a little black dress.

I pulled my long hair into a ponytail. I hardly ever wear makeup, and applying it took up a good chunk of time.

I went back into my bedroom to get a pair of shoes, and saw Karma sitting on the bed.

"What do you think?" I spun around a couple times so she could get the whole picture.

She yawned, stretched, and laid back down the bed. It was evident she wasn't impressed.

Nate was right on time, and we drove up the coast, to a nice restaurant in Algonac. We got a table looking out over the St. Clair River, and enjoyed watching the large ice flows travel south while we munched on our appetizers.

Dinner was amazing, and the conversation was light, not forced. We both struggled to stay away from the topic of murder and just enjoy the evening.

"So…" I leaned forward and rested my hands on the table. "I hardly know anything about you."

"I'm pretty simple, really. I grew up in Texas. My dad owns a ranch. When I graduated high school, I wanted adventure, so I joined the Navy."

That explained the cowboy boots.

"How did you end up becoming a cop?"

"I always wanted to be in some kind of law enforcement, so after boot camp I went through their training. When I left the Navy, I joined a small police department. When a detective opportunity opened up here, I jumped at the chance."

I gave him a coy smile. "I'm glad you did."

"Me, too." He reached across the table and squeezed my hand.

We spent the rest of the evening talking and enjoying our dinner. After we ate, we put on our coats and walked hand-in-hand along the restaurant pier.

When we got back to my house, Nate walked me up to the door and gave me the perfect first-date kiss. We said goodnight, and I locked the door behind me.

The euphoria of one of the best first dates I've ever had lasted until my cell phone pinged and I saw Adrianna's number.

"Hey, what's up?"

"Zoey, I locked myself out of the house. I'm on the front porch, and the same car has circled the block three times. Help me!"

"Sit tight. I'm on the way."

I looked up the number of a locksmith that does emergency calls, gave him Adrianna's address, and ran out of the house, to my Jeep. On the way to her house, I prayed that she hadn't been abducted by the time I got there.

Thankfully, she was sitting on a chair on her porch, and the locksmith pulled in behind me. A few minutes later, we were in her house.

"Thanks for coming over," she said.

"No problem. I'm just glad you're okay. I'm going to go. See you later."

"Wait!" She held out a key to her house. "Take this in case I lock myself out again. Please?"

I took the key out of her hand. "Okay. Thanks."

I put her key in the cupholder and drove home.

Before I went to bed, I put Adrianna's key on an old key ring I'd found in the junk drawer. The key ring had a label on it, so I put Adrianna's name on it, and tucked it into my purse.

I got changed into my pajamas, and fell into a sound sleep, with Karma curled up beside me.

In the morning, I curled up in my office chair with a cup of coffee, and got back to work on the Jane Doe file. In less than an hour, I'd made the final connection, and knew, with relative certainty, who she was. I printed out all the information, along with people Agent Phillips should contact to confirm, and sealed it in an envelope. I then tucked copies into my file, marked it closed, and filed it away.

I texted Agent Phillips and told him that Mabel had a delivery for him. He texted back and set up a time for later this morning.

Good. That meant I had plenty of time to take my shower and get ready to go.

I opened the genealogy site and checked Bea's tree to see if any hints had turned up. There were many.

Excellent! This may not be as hard as I'd originally had thought.

I managed to fill in a lot of the Perkins's line. Millicent Jenkins Perkins was her great-grandmother, and Elijah Perkins her great-grandfather.

Bea had wanted me to concentrate on the British side of her family, but in my mind, there's no point in doing a job if you're not going to do it completely.

I filled in more of her family tree until it was time to get ready to meet Agent Phillips. The Jenkins's line was filling in nicely, and as I shut down my computer, I was satisfied with my progress.

Bea probably wouldn't be real impressed, because I hadn't been able to link her to nobility yet. But time would tell.

After getting ready, I drove to the cemetery and placed the envelope on Mabel's grave, then sat in my truck to wait until Agent Phillips arrived. Ten minutes later, he pulled into the cemetery and parked.

He got out and walked toward the gravestone, with his head on the swivel.

I shook my head. *So paranoid.*

After he left, I pulled out of the cemetery and went back home. I felt restless, so I decided to take a walk through town. When I got to the bookstore, I saw Frank moving around inside. It was Sunday, and the store wouldn't open until noon.

He saw me and hurried to unlock the store for me.

"How's it going, Frank?" I shut the door behind me.

"Couldn't be better!" He smiled. "People love Holmes, and business has increased ten percent since he's been here."

"He's an animal, Frank, not a marketing ploy." I sighed.

Holmes jumped up onto the counter, and I stroked his back. He lay down and rolled over so I could rub his tummy.

Frank scratched him behind the ears, and Holmes was in kitty heaven.

"I know. And I have to admit, he's good company." The smile left his face. "I never realized how lonely I'd been until I got Holmes."

We spent a few more minutes talking, and he said his date with Bea had gone wonderfully, and that he was escorting her to church this morning. I was glad to hear that both of them had found someone they hadn't known they'd needed.

"See you later, Frank." I waved goodbye as I left the store.

When I pulled into the driveway, Adrianna was just getting out of her car, parked in front of my house. She rushed toward me, threw her arms around me, and burst into tears.

"Thank God you're home."

I eased out of her hug and started to walk up to the front porch.

"What's wrong, Adrianna?"

Not that I didn't know. But I wanted to hear it from her.

She took off her coat and put it over the arm of the couch before sitting.

"You heard about the other body, right?"

"I heard." I sat in the living room chair across from her.

"What can I do?" She held out her hands in front of her, palms up.

"Why don't you try telling the truth." I'd lost all patience with her.

"Huh?" She looked at me.

"Adrianna, everyone knows you're not being completely honest, and that you're holding something back. And while you may be too scared or embarrassed to come clean, innocent women continue to be slaughtered. If you really want all this to stop, then you better start talking, before you're his next victim. Because whether you want to admit it or not, that's the endgame here."

She buried her face in her hands, and her shoulders shook as she sobbed.

Maybe I pushed her too far.

After a few minutes she looked up at me with tears in her eyes.

"Someone other than Chad has been stalking me for the past two years."

Finally! Now we're getting somewhere. "Who?"

"I DON'T KNOW." SHE shrugged.

How could she not know? Here we go again.

"You must have some idea. I mean, another old boyfriend, co-worker?"

She threw up her hands. "I honestly have no idea. It started after my mother died."

"I'm sorry about your mom. Was she sick?" I got up and went into the kitchen to get us something to drink.

"No. She was killed in a car accident." Adrianna wiped her eyes with the back of her hand.

"How horrible for you and your family."

I set her drink down on the coffee table in front of her, and made myself comfortable in the overstuffed chair next to the couch.

"Thank you. Anyway, shortly after the funeral, I started finding dead animals on the front porch. Squirrels, rabbits, birds. They'd been mutilated."

"Ewww." I wrinkled my nose. "Did you report it to the police?"

She shook her head. "No. I thought it was just the work of a stray cat or something."

I nodded. It seemed plausible. But what was her aversion to the police?

"There was all that going on, and then I think I was being followed." She took a gulp of her drink.

"What makes you think that?"

"I started seeing the same car all the time. A black sedan. Foreign, I think. It would be everywhere. Parked in front of the house, at the stores, my work." She looked up at me.

"Did you ever see anyone in it?" *A black foreign sedan. Could have been anyone. They're not exactly a rare breed.*

"Not clearly." She furrowed her brow. "The windows were tinted, but I knew there was someone in it. Understand?"

I nodded.

"Then the notes started showing up on my truck windshield, mostly. Just like a sticky note or something." A far-away look crossed her face as she remembered. "They would say things like, *Sorry about your Mom.* Things like that."

"Okay. And?"

I still didn't understand how or why these scared her if they were that simple.

"Then I started getting phone calls from unknown numbers. I'd answer, and no one would say anything. But I could hear them breathing." She shivered. "Sometimes that song, 'I'll Be Watching You,' would be playing in the background."

Okay, that was disturbing. I remembered being stalked by Seth, and how scary that was.

"Did you tell the police?"

"No." She shook her head. "I sold the house and moved away from Paytonville."

I nodded.

Paytonville was in the center of the state. She'd moved a good distance away, for sure.

"What about your Dad? Did you tell him?"

"My father isn't around. He disappeared when I was six."

"Disappeared?" *That's interesting.*

"I don't remember much about it—I was so little. When I got older, I would ask my mom about it, but would get a different answer each time."

I could tell it still bothered her.

"Did you ever try to find him?"

Her lack of curiosity irked me to no end, and I struggled to keep myself in check.

"No. I didn't see the point. Anyway, everywhere I moved, it would be fine for a few months, and then the stalker would find me again, and it would start all over." She stared at me, and I could see the fear in her eyes. "The dead animals, the notes…but now. Now it's gotten worse."

"You think?" I glared at her. "Do you have any of the notes he's sent?"

"No! I tore them to shreds and threw them away." She looked at me like I was crazy. "Why would I keep them?"

"To give to the police." I got up and started to pace around the room. "Have you seen the black car?"

"Yes. Almost every day. I'm sure it's the same one."

"Have you gotten the license plate number?"

"No. I never thought of that. I'm just so scared." A tear ran down her cheek.

I couldn't blame her for being afraid. Anyone would be. Honestly, I didn't think this girl had an ounce of common sense in her whole body. But enough was enough. I picked up my cell phone and dialed Nate.

"Who are you calling?" She seemed panicked.

"The police. You are going to tell them everything."

"But he'll kill me?"

"Who will?"

"The stalker. He said if I went to the police, he'd kill me."

"When did he say this?"

Nate answered, and I told him to come over, and why.

"He called me two days ago. He was using something to distort his voice. It sounded electronic. But he said that he'd kill me if I told the police." She started to shake.

"Do you still have the message?"

"No. I erased it."

"Adrianna…" I'd never been so exasperated in my life. "Don't do that again. Save everything. Okay? Detective Emerson is on the way here. I'll be right here with you, okay?"

She hung her head and mumbled her agreement.

I saw Nate pull up, and let him in. He looked surprised to see Adrianna there, so I filled him in.

Nate sat in the chair next to the couch, and I sat next to Adrianna and held her hand.

"Start from the beginning, please, Miss Martinelli." His eyes were hard, and his voice firm.

He was pissed, and I couldn't really blame him.

"I'm going to record this interview with your permission." He sat a digital recorder on the coffee table and turned it on.

She nodded.

For the next two hours, Adrianna told her story and Nate asked lots of questions. When they'd finished, Nate stood and stretched, and Adrianna excused herself to use the bathroom.

Nate and I exchanged looks.

"I'm going to go. I have a lot to follow-up on." He walked toward the door.

Adrianna joined us in the living room.

"Miss Martinelli, if you see this car again, you are to call me immediately. Understand?"

"I will." Her shoulders slumped. "I'm sorry."

After Nate left, Adrianna claimed she was exhausted and was going home. I walked her to the door.

"Call me if you need anything." I gave her a hug. "Even if you're just scared. I'm only a couple minutes away. I'll be right there."

She hugged me back. "Thanks, Zoey. I will."

I went onto the front porch and watched her get into her car and drive away. I glanced up and down the street, waiting for a black sedan to follow her, but didn't see one.

When I went back into the house, I headed to my office to write down all that information I'd learned, and my mind was racing so fast I had to force myself to slow down so I could form a clear thought. Since I wasn't sure Nate was going to take the same course of action, I settled in and got to work.

In less than five minutes, I had Adrianna's birth certificate. Her parents were Antonio and Maria Martinelli.

Good. Just what I needed.

I jumped onto a newspaper website and typed in Maria Martinelli's name. Several newspaper articles came up from a little over two years ago. She'd been killed in a hit-and-run accident.

Hmm. Adrianna had left out that part.

Witnesses to the accident said that she'd been hit by a dark blue or black pickup truck that'd had a big push bar on the front.

How convenient.

The article went on to say that the police were still investigating.

The other articles were from different newspapers, and pretty much all had the same information. I made a note of the dates and other information, and sat back in my chair while the article was printing.

As I re-read the article, my skin started to tingle, and the hair on the back of my neck stood up. That usually meant something wasn't right. Could Adrianna's mother have been murdered?

There was only one way to find out. I tried searching online for old police files in Paytonville, where the accident happened. But, as with many small towns, their files weren't yet digitized.

I then searched for Adrianna's father, Antonio. Three articles popped up, but one of the headlines caught my attention. It read: *Local Man Missing Presumed Dead.*

What the hell? I need to get ahold of that file.

typed out two Freedom of Information Act letters—one for Adrianna's mother's file, and one for her father. After signing them, I faxed them to the numbers I'd found online. Hopefully it wouldn't take too long to get copies.

Police records are normally a matter of public record. But because both of them could technically be considered open files, there was a risk I wouldn't be able to get them.

Karma wandered into my office and sat in front of the murder board staring up at it, turning her head as she looked back and forth. She reached out a paw and batted at one of the red twine ends I'd forgotten to clip when I was connecting things together, then turned around and meowed at me.

"What?" I turned around in my chair to look at her. "Did I miss something?"

She gave the board one more glance before letting out a heavy sigh and jumping up on my desk. She curled up on her blanket and proceeded to give herself a good cleaning.

I sat and stared at the murder board for a long time, but I couldn't see anything I'd missed. Damn cat had succeeded in making me paranoid.

I shook my head and turned back around to get to work on another FBI file. This one was of a John Doe who'd been found on the upper peninsula of Michigan. His body had been found in 1987, but the coroner believed he'd been dead for at least two or three years before that. Foul play was suspected, but the file didn't elaborate.

Thank goodness that coroner had the presence of mind to preserve a tooth from the victim, in hopes that one day technology would catch up. The DNA had been taken from the tooth, and they'd been able to extract enough for a decent sample.

As I read the file further, I learned he'd been found wearing military-style boots, and camouflage pants and shirt. The FBI had done a facial reconstruction, and I studied the picture for a few moments.

It always disturbed me on some level to see the face of the victim. It made my job more personal—less generic. This was someone's child. Maybe someone's brother, husband, or father. He'd been so young—twenty-three to thirty-five.

A lump developed in my throat, and I had to close the file. I took a few moments to compose myself.

The only chance this poor man had of receiving any type of justice was for me to do my job and find out who he was. So I grabbed a tissue out of the box on my desk, wiped my eyes, and settled in for the long haul. I wasn't going to stop until I knew who he was.

Three hours later, I knew I was close. My eyes burned from staring at the computer screen, and a headache had developed behind my left eye. I stopped to take a couple aspirin and put in eye drops.

As I passed the living room to head back down the hall to my office, out of the corner of my eye, I thought I saw someone standing by the large oak tree that stood between the sidewalk and the road.

I stopped short and took a closer look. Someone was definitely there, but they were partially hidden by the massive trunk of the old tree, and I couldn't see who it was.

I walked over to the sectional and crouched down on one of the cushions, facing the window. Then I peered over the back to see if they would show themselves.

Should I go out and confront them? It could be Chad. Was he stalking me now? No, that was nuts. Stop. It's probably nothing. Maybe I should call the police. But tell them what? They haven't done anything wrong.

I just had to quit being paranoid.

As I stared, Jason emerged from behind the tree, and with one last look at the house, trudged across the street and got into his truck. He backed out of his driveway, gunned the engine, and sped down the street.

What the hell?

The entire situation left me unnerved. In my heart, I knew Jason would never hurt me. But my mind wasn't so sure.

I turned away from the window and curled up into a ball on the couch. I felt violated, and scared.

I got up, and after setting the alarm, headed back to my office. I needed a break from trying to find this poor man's family.

I turned around and looked back at the murder board.

Then I saw it—I didn't have any red twine connecting the victims.

"Is that what you were trying to tell me?" I looked at Karma.

She opened her eyes and gave me a withering look before going back to sleep.

"Okay, then."

I decided to delve deeper into the pasts of the two women who'd been murdered. Maybe there was a link between them and Adrianna.

The popularity of the Internet wasn't good for personal privacy or security. But for people like me, it was a virtual goldmine of information.

After a lot of searching and backtracking, I was able to find a tenuous link between them. They all belonged to the same dating sites. Then again, so did a lot of other people. But at least it was a place to start.

Maybe they all had contact with the same person at some point. There was no way to find that out without hacking into their accounts. While I was perfectly capable of doing that, it was unethical.

But maybe there was another way...

I yawned and stretched in my desk chair. I'd been sitting there for hours, and my back hurt. Everything was going to have to wait until tomorrow. Enough was enough for one day. I was tired and hungry.

It was after 7:00 p.m. before I traveled into town. Instead of Gil's, I decided to eat at the Blue Bass. It was more upscale, and the food was delicious. The restaurant is in a building that used to be a pharmacy. The owners had left the original wood floors, and with the open, painted vent work, it had a loft-like appearance.

The hostess led me to a small table at the front, by the bay windows. I ordered a glass of wine and perused the daily specials. Once I'd decided, I put the menu aside and saw some historic photographs of Hope Harbor under the glass top of the table.

These pictures depicted what is now the park, but in the late 1800s, was a bustling shipping port. There were large docks, schooners, and men loading and unloading the ships.

I sipped the wine the waitress delivered and ordered the salmon before staring out the window to the street. People were walking their dogs and shopping. Everyone seemed to be coupled up, and a profound sense of loneliness wrapped around me. Here I was again, eating dinner alone. It seemed as if I chased away everyone who tried to get close to me. Jason. And he wasn't the first one. I couldn't even remember the last close relationship I'd had.

As I sat there drowning in self-pity, I felt someone touch my shoulder. I looked up and saw Nate standing there. His handsome face looked as tired as I felt, and his well-defined jaw was set.

"Want company?" He sat in the wooden chair across from me. "I hate to eat alone."

"You get used to it." I shrugged.

He raised an eyebrow. "Bad day?"

"Not really. You?" I tried to shake my melancholic mood.

"Nah. Just frustrated with this case."

The waitress approached, and Nate ordered a beer and dinner. I nodded. "I found a link between the victims and Adrianna."

He closed the menu and looked at me. "You have my undivided attention."

I told him about all the women being members of the same dating sites.

"I know it's not much, but it's something, right?" I looked at him, expectantly.

"It's something. We've talked to most of the guys Sienna had contact with. I could cross-reference them with Natalie. We have her laptop. The trick would be for Adrianna to give up that information."

He was right. I wasn't sure Adrianna would admit to belonging to the dating sites, let alone tell anyone know who's she been talking to.

"True," I said. "But if you find a link between the first two victims, Sienna and Natalie, maybe I could talk to Adrianna and persuade her to give up that information.

"I can always subpoena it. But I wouldn't do that until I can link the other two women to the same man."

Made sense.

"Now, no more talk of murder," he said. "Let's just try to relax and enjoy our time together." He reached across the table and gave my hand a gentle squeeze.

I squeezed back. "Let's."

Over dinner, we talked about our lives, and I found myself telling him things I rarely tell anyone—such as my mother's alcoholism, and my father's suicide. He listened intently, and shared stories from his family. Sounded as if he'd had a much happier childhood than I had. But it didn't matter. Everyone has their own story.

We left the restaurant around nine, and he insisted on walking me home. I didn't put up much of a protest, and before heading to my house, we walked hand-in-hand through town. He asked a lot of questions about the town, the people, and the different shops, and I was more than happy to tell him what I knew.

Before long, we ended up on my front porch, kissing goodnight. I was reluctant to let him leave, but didn't try to stop him. I lingered on the porch and watched him walk down the sidewalk, out of sight.

As I started to shut the front door, I noticed Jason peeking out from the blinds on his front window. With a sigh, I locked the door and set the alarm. The evening with Nate had been nice, but I was bone tired. Not to mention, mentally and emotionally drained. I needed sleep—lots of it.

Since tomorrow was Saturday, I planned on skipping my run and sleeping in.

The pealing of the doorbell jolted me out of a sound sleep, at 6:00 a.m.

"What the hell!" I threw off the covers and stumbled to shut off the alarm.

Without even bothering to see who it was, I opened the front door.

"In the name of all that is holy, this better be good!"

Nate was standing there with a file folder and two coffees from Gil's. He burst out laughing.

"Good morning to you, too." He walked by me and into the kitchen.

I had no choice but to shut the door and follow him. He handed me my coffee, and I glared at him over the rim as I took my first sip.

"Don't you people sleep?" I plopped down on one the stools at the kitchen island.

He opened the file he'd brought with him. "I found three men that Sienna and Natalie were both talking to in the weeks before they were murdered."

"Really? That's great."

I was impressed. He must have stayed up most the night looking for any link.

I leaned over his shoulder to get a peek at the names on his list, but he slammed the file closed.

"I can't let you see the file. And I may get fired for this, but you can come with me when I talk to Adrianna. She seems to trust you."

That seemed fair. Frustrating, but fair.

"Okay." I sighed. "When do you want to go?"

"Why don't you get dressed, and I'll take you to breakfast. We'll go to Adrianna's after that."

"Deal!" I started down the hall to my bedroom. "Can you feed Karma, please?"

As I ransacked my closet looking for something to wear, I heard him opening cupboards trying to find the cat food. He must have found it, because he started to talk to her, and I heard the sound of a spoon hit the edge of her glass dish.

Smiling to myself, I took a quick shower and threw on a pair of jeans and super-soft pink cashmere sweater. I pulled my hair into a ponytail, and even put on a little makeup.

Nate gave me an approving look as I joined him in the kitchen. He helped me into my coat and opened the truck door for me. A few minutes later, we were tucked into a booth at Gil's, deciding what to order.

We kept the conversation over breakfast away from the murders. The restaurant was crowded, and gossip spread through Hope Harbor like wildfire. Instead, Nate asked me about my work. I told him about the job I was doing for the FBI, without going into too many specifics. He seemed impressed, and asked a lot of good questions.

He paid the bill, and we headed out onto the sidewalk. He'd had to park down the street, and just as we'd started toward his truck, Jason appeared out of the darkness and blocked our path.

"We need to talk." He grabbed my hand and pulled me toward him.

"STOP IT!" I pulled my hand away. "I don't want to talk to you. Just leave me alone and quit spying on me."

Jason took a step toward me, but Nate moved in front of me.

"This isn't the time for this," he said. "Leave her alone. If she wants to talk to you, she'll come to you. Okay?" He rested his hand on the butt of his gun, holstered on his belt.

"This isn't over." Jason stepped off the sidewalk and headed across the street.

Nate turned to face me. "Are you okay? Why didn't you tell me he's been spying on you? You need to report this."

I shook my head. "No, it's okay."

But it wasn't okay. He never used to be like this. *What the hell?*

"Let's get to Adrianna's." I started down the sidewalk, and Nate caught up with me.

He put his hand on the small of my back as we walked to his truck.

When we arrived at Adrianna's and rang the bell, she opened the door and gave us a shocked expression, which she quickly tried to hide behind a smile. As she escorted us into the living room, she kept fidgeting with her hair, and didn't seem to know what to do with her hands. I chalked it up to Nate being there.

We sat in the living room—Nate and I on the couch, and Adrianna in a chair.

"Miss Martinelli, we think we found a link between the two women who were murdered and yourself. But we need to confirm it. Can you help us do that?"

"If I can." She looked at me.

I nodded.

"We know that both women belonged to a couple of online dating sites," Nate said. "The same ones you belong to."

Adrianna's eyes became wide. She must not have realized Nate could get hold of such information. Or was it something else?

"We need to know if you've ever spoken to a Daniel Parchinelli, Marcus Anderson, or Peter Billings." He looked at Adrianna, expectantly.

"I'm not sure. Maybe."

"Can you please check for us?" His voice became stern.

He was getting frustrated, and I couldn't blame him. Adrianna frustrated the hell out of me with her half-truths and evasiveness.

Her shoulders slumped, and she seemed to deflate into her chair.

"It could take a bit."

"That's okay," Nate said. "We can wait. Or if you prefer, I can subpoena the records directly from the dating sites."

He was playing hardball, and I liked it.

A look of horror crossed Adrianna's face.

"I'll be right back." Adrianna disappeared down the hallway toward the bedrooms.

She returned a moment later with her laptop, and put it on the kitchen table before sitting in one of the dining chairs. Nate crossed the living room to stand beside her, and looked over her shoulder. Adrianna squirmed in her chair. Clearly, Nate being able to read her computer screen made her uneasy. I resisted the urge not to smile like a Cheshire cat as I got off the couch and stood next to Nate.

Adrianna looked over her shoulder and gave me a pleading look, but I wasn't going to help her this time. It was vital Nate had all the information he could get.

He gave her the name of the dating site, and Adrianna logged in and went to her messages. As far as I could tell, she'd only had contact with one of the men—Daniel Parchinelli.

I took out my cell phone and made note of the name. Nate shot me a dirty look when he saw what I was typing, but I stared him down and wrinkled my nose at him.

"Thank you, Miss Martinelli. You've been very helpful. We'll be in touch. You ready?" He looked at me.

I nodded.

"What do you think?" he said, as we headed toward my house.

"I don't know what to think." I shrugged. "Maybe I'll have a better opinion once I check out Mister Parchinelli."

"You don't have to do that. I'll take care of it. And why am I wasting my breath? You're going to do it, anyway." He sighed.

I smiled, but remained quiet the rest of the ride home.

Nate just dropped me off, which was fine. He had to follow up on the new lead.

As much as I wanted to get to work on finding out more about the new mystery man, I had to get some work done.

I grabbed a soda out of the fridge and retreated to my office, where I turned my murder board around so I couldn't see it and become distracted.

An hour later, I finally had a connection between the poor man found dead in Northern Michigan, and a family. It was something. Two of the people I believed were related in some way were still living, and it didn't take long for me to use a couple of databases to track down their contact information.

When I'd finished with my report, I texted Agent Phillips told him I needed to talk to him, and that I had information about one of the cases. He texted me back, asking me to meet him in a couple hours, at the building we met at before in Detroit.

As I drove toward the freeway to head down to Detroit, I thought about the events of the morning with Adrianna. I needed to figure out a way to crack her shell and make her put her guard down so she'd trust me more.

I glanced in my rearview mirror and saw Jason's truck settle in behind me. I sped up and waited until the last second to swerve onto the freeway headed south. I felt bad about cutting off another car in the ramp lane, but I didn't have any other choice. Jason wasn't quick enough, and missed the entrance ramp.

A little while later, I pulled into the parking lot of the building and parked in the back this time. I walked around to the front of the building and knocked. Agent Phillips let me in, and went to the conference room. I stopped at the door because there was another man in the room.

"Zoey, this is Agent Christopher Pellegrino. He works with me on these files. If for some reason you can't reach me, you can contact Christopher."

The man stood, gave me a warm smile, and extended his hand.

"Nice to meet you. Agent Phillips has told me what a valuable asset you are to him."

We shook hands.

"Thanks. Nice to meet you as well."

He was young. Probably not much older than me. His blond hair was cut military short, and he had kind blue eyes.

We all sat at the table, and I handed Agent Phillips the file.

"Here's the file on a John Doe. I think if you contact one of these people, they can identify who this poor man is." I showed them my notes.

"Great work." Agent Pellegrino got up from his chair and picked up the file. "I'll get started on this right away. Here's my card, just in case you need to reach me." He handed me his card, then and left the room and shut the door behind him.

Agent Phillips turned his attention to me. "What did you want to talk about?"

Maybe this was a bad idea. I didn't want to get Jason into trouble at work.

"Has Jason been acting like himself lately?"

Agent Phillips sat back in his chair and appeared to be taken aback by my question.

"I haven't seen him a lot. We're working on different cases. But now that you mention it, he does seem a little off."

I leaned forward. "Like how?"

"He's been short-tempered, and seems to be anxious about something. It's probably just the job. It does that to you. I know he's mentioned getting headaches lately, but I'm sure it's just because he's stressed. I get them, too."

"Probably. Thanks." I rose to leave.

Maybe Agent Phillips was right. Jason's job was extremely stressful. But that still didn't explain his archaic and traditional attitudes when it comes to women.

"Why do you ask?" Phillips was standing with his hand on the doorknob, blocking my exit.

"He's just been acting weird." I shrugged. "He's become controlling, and has said he wants me to be what he calls a *normal woman*, whatever that means."

Agent Phillips reached out and briefly put his hand on my arm. "I'm sorry, Zoey."

"Then I told him we were over. And since then, he's been spying on me." I looked up at him.

I knew I'd probably said too much, but once I'd started talking, the words just tumbled out on their own.

"Stalking?" A stern look crossed Agent Phillips face.

I shook my head. "I wouldn't call it stalking. He's just been keeping tabs on me."

"Do you want me to talk to him."

The thought horrified me.

"No. Please don't say a word. I'm sure he'll get over it."

"Keep me informed. If it doesn't stop, action is going to have to be taken. Understand?" He put both hands on my shoulders, and burned his dark gaze into mine.

"I will. Thanks." I resisted the urge to shrug his hands off my shoulders.

"Why don't I let you out the back. You'll have less far to walk." He released me from his grip.

"Great." *How does he know I parked in the back?*

Agent Phillips opened the back door and looked around before allowing me to exit.

"Take care. Talk soon."

"Later." I went to my truck.

Before pulling off, I looked at the building's exterior. There were security cameras tucked under the eaves in each corner. Nothing unusual about that. Lots of buildings have security cameras. But that answered my question.

As I drove home, I thought about Agent Pellegrino. It was the first time Agent Phillips had ever introduced me to another agent. *Interesting.*

But other than the two of them, there'd been no one else in the building, just like the last time. I couldn't help but wonder what that building was used for.

I ran a few errands, and by the time I got home it was almost dinner time. As I pulled into the driveway, I saw Frank Dixon's car in Bea's driveway. I smiled as I unloaded my groceries. It was nice to see Frank and Bea enjoying each other's company.

Once I had the groceries put away, I retreated to my office. I turned the murder board back around and studied it. It was time to find out more about Mr. Parchinelli.

It didn't take long to find a picture of Daniel Parchinelli on social media, and I added him to the board and connected him to Adrianna and the murder victims. Now I just had to find out more about him.

He lived in Ferndale, which was less than ten miles from the cities the two victims lived in, but a little over forty miles from Hope Harbor. I was pretty sure that was an important fact, but I didn't know why.

With a little more research, I learned that Mr. Parchinelli had an interesting criminal record. He'd been arrested twice for domestic abuse, but both times, the charges had been dropped. He'd also been charged and convicted of assault, but accepted a plea deal and ended up being sentenced to four years of probation.

He worked as a construction supervisor and appeared to be making good money. His credit wasn't great, but it wasn't horrible either. In recent months, it appeared that he'd been trying to improve his standing.

He also owned an older model pickup truck with a cap on it. That's not unusual for someone who works in construction. It also made for a convenient place to murder women, which could explain why the primary murder scenes hadn't been found.

It was late, and I was getting ready to go to bed, when the doorbell rang. I peeked out the small window and saw Adrianna.

"Come in. Is something wrong?" *What now?*

She sat on the couch, and after shrugging off her coat, looked up at me.

"I left something out this morning."

I sighed. *Not again.* I felt my temper trying to raise its ugly head, but forced myself to remain calm.

"What?"

"I was so flustered with the detective looking over my shoulder. I've talked to another one of those men, but it was on a different dating site. I thought he was just asking about the one site." She hung her head.

"Which one?" I plopped down in a living room chair.

She finally looked up at me. "Marcus Anderson. But he seems like a really nice guy. It can't be him."

"That's what they said about Ted Bundy, too."

She furrowed her brow. "Huh?"

"He was a serial killer. Everyone said he was a nice guy. Did you call Nate?"

"No. Can you tell him? I'm afraid he's going to yell at me."

I wanted to yell at her.

"That should be the least of your worries. You'll be lucky if he doesn't arrest you for obstructing a police investigation."

A look of horror crossed her face. "He can do that?"

"Yes. And honestly, Adrianna, I wouldn't blame him if he did."
I stood.

This visit was over.

"You need to print out all the messages both men have sent you, and give them to the police. Understand?"

She stood and put on her coat. I opened the door for her and gave her a curt goodbye before locking the door behind her. Then I shut all the blinds and locked up the house.

Marcus Anderson would have to wait until the morning. I'd had enough for one day.

I shut down my computer and set the alarm before heading to bed.

It didn't dawn on me until the next morning that I hadn't told Nate about Adrianna's visit last night, and the new information she'd given me. I texted him and poured myself another cup of coffee before heading into my office.

I needed to get some work done on Bea's genealogy. Since it was the weekend, I didn't feel as guilty about not working on the stack of FBI files waiting for me in my cabinet.

I decided to see what else I could find out about the Perkin's family, on her maternal line. I started with Millicent. She and Elijah had four children, before Elijah died at the age of thirty-five.

One of their children, Mary, caught my eye, only because there were court records attached to her. A quick search brought up a lot of documents to go through. I clicked on one of them and found out that she'd been arrested on suspicion of prostitution. The arresting officer was Deputy Chief Mario Martinelli. He'd told the judge that she had been found drunk, with her petticoats over her head.

Oh, no! How am I going to tell this to Bea? Maybe I'll just print it out and let her read it.

Poor Bea. Her ancestor was far from the nobility she had hoped to learn about.

I switched gears and discovered that Inspector Martinelli had been high up in the police department.

Something didn't seem right. Why would an inspector of police waste his time arresting prostitutes. Wasn't that plain old Bobby-on-the-beat stuff? I didn't know anything about the police culture in England during the Victorian era, but I knew who did—Rodger Frost.

As much as I wanted to call him, I decided it could wait until next week. Didn't want to bother him on the weekend. I printed out as much information as I could find, put it in a labeled folder, and set it aside.

It was time to dig into the life of Marcus Anderson—the other man the two victims and Adrianna had all talked to on a dating site.

I found a picture of him on social media, printed it out and put it on my murder board, next to Daniel Parchinelli's photograph. I got out my ball of red string and began to connect both men to Adrianna and the other two women.

Karma came into the room and kept leaping to try to grab the dangling end of the string.

"Stop it!" I started to laugh.

I cut a piece of string off the roll and gave it to her to play with so I could finish making the connections in peace. She took the piece of string and disappeared down the hallway, dragging it behind her. I thought I'd now be able to get some work done, but she reappeared a few minutes later and curled up on the blanket at the corner of my desk.

After about an hour of research, I concluded that Marcus Anderson was squeaky clean. He didn't have a criminal record. He paid his bills, and didn't appear to be involved in the drama of social media. In fact, most of his posts had to do with the hockey team he played on in the winter, and the baseball team he pitched for in the warmer months. He was a certified public accountant, and I checked him out with the licensing board. He was in good standing and had never had a complaint filed against him.

As much as I hated to pre-judge people without having met them, Daniel Parchinelli appeared to be more of a viable suspect than Marcus Anderson. Nonetheless, I left Marcus's picture on my murder board. I'd been wrong about people before—Jason, for example.

So my two main suspects were Chad Eastwick and Daniel Parchinelli. Chad had the best motive, and a nasty temper. But Daniel had a criminal history.

I glanced out the window and saw the sun shining on early spring day in Hope Harbor. I decided to take advantage of it and get outside for some fresh air.

I changed into warmer clothes and hiking boots before running next door to Bea's and telling her I was taking Atlas out for a romp. She seemed relieved to have a break, and the German Shepherd was giddy with excitement as I loaded him into my Jeep.

It wasn't as warm as I thought it was, so I cranked up the heat and rolled the back window down so Atlas could stick his head out of it—one of his favorite things. I had to laugh when I glanced in one of my side mirrors and saw him with his tongue out, blowing in the wind. He was in his glory. I knew exactly where we were going—the witch cemetery. For some reason, since I'd been hired by the historical society to research it last year, I couldn't get the place out of my mind.

I pulled off onto the shoulder. I probably could have pulled into the driveway of the old Rockman house—which Jason was renovating—but I didn't want him to know I was there. He'd bought the house a few months ago because it had belonged to his ancestors.

I put Atlas on his leash until we were in the woods and away from the road. Then I let him go. While he ran off to explore, I followed at a more leisurely pace. The dead leaves on the ground made a soft carpet for me to walk on, and I relaxed and let my thoughts roam free.

The air smelled clean and fresh, and the sunlight wafting through the barren branches of the trees cast shadows that seemed to dance along the ground. This had been a good idea.

Within a few minutes, the woods gave way to the old cemetery. The tombstones—most of them more than a century old—stood as silent witnesses, as a testament that the people buried there had once mattered. Most of the women buried in the cemetery had been accused of witchcraft. While there'd never been witch trials, when the women died, they weren't allowed to be buried in the sacred ground of the town cemetery. The thought of what these women and their families must have endured still hurt my heart.

Atlas came thundering out of the woods and joined me in the cemetery. He was panting, and burrs from the underbrush were stuck in his thick coat. I called him over to me and started to pick the debris out of his fur. I realized this was an exercise in futility, because we had over a half-mile back through the woods to the truck. But it seemed like the thing to do.

I decided to minimize the burr situation by putting him on his lead before we started back. As we walked, I relished the sounds of the squirrels climbing up and down the trees and scurrying through the leaves. Some of the birds were starting to return from their winter homes, and they sat in the high branches, announcing their arrival and that springtime was soon upon us. I breathed in the earthy, musky smells, allowing myself to truly enjoy the moment.

Atlas began to growl, and his jowls curled up, revealing his large, sharp teeth.

"What's wrong, boy?" I stopped to listen for any sound that was out of place.

Atlas positioned himself in front of me, and the hair on his neck raised. He lowered his body lowered, as if prepared to attack. My body tensed in response to his defensive stance.

In the distance, I finally heard what he'd reacted to—someone walking through the dried leaves and pushing through the underbrush. I looked around and saw a large man coming through the woods, toward me.

It wasn't until he got closer to me that I realized it was Jason, who stopped about eight feet away from me when he noticed the large dog at my side. Because of Atlas's coloring, he blended into the browns and blacks of the hibernating woods, and was hard to spot.

"Hi," he said. "I was working on the house and saw someone in the woods, from one of the upstairs windows."

That was a lie. It was impossible for him to have seen me from the house, even when I was in the cemetery. He must have spotted my truck when he pulled into the driveway of the Rockman place.

"How's the house coming along?" I made no attempt to make Atlas stand down.

"Good. You want to see it?"

Not on your life. My chest tightened, and my stomach was in knots.

"Not today. But thanks."

"Hey, remember the boxes of stuff I told you about from the Rockman's," he said, "in the attic of the house?"

I nodded.

"I'll put them in my truck and drop them off later. Maybe there's stuff in there that will help you with your research."

"That would be great. Thanks."

"I'll walk you back to your Jeep." He took a step toward me.

Atlas growled and showed his teeth.

Jason stopped. "That's some dog."

"He is." I put my hand on Atlas's back, but didn't discipline him for growling.

I'd never been so happy to have him with me as I was right then.

"Atlas and I can find our way. Thanks." I turned and started to walk in the opposite direction.

Atlas came with me, but kept looking back at Jason. When we were a fair distance away from him, I stopped and crouched down to give Atlas a hug.

"Thanks, boy," I whispered in his ear.

He nuzzled my face.

When we got home, I brought him in the house and gave him a big bowl of water and a few treats. Before taking him home, I grabbed the printout with the information I'd found earlier.

"Hey, Bea!" I opened the front door to let the dog in.

I really wished she would get in the habit of locking her doors.

"In the kitchen!" She turned around to look at me.

Atlas walked over to his bed and plopped down.

Bea laughed. "Guess you wore him out. Thank goodness."

"I did."

"Fantastic!" She gave me a hug.

"Bea, I found out some information on one of your ancestors." I put the paper down on the table. "I'm afraid it's not the news you were hoping to hear."

She dried her hands on a dish towel and picked up the paper. As she read, her eyes grew wide and her mouth dropped open.

"Oh, my stars! I have to sit down." She sank into one of the chairs at the dining table.

"I'm sorry, Bea." I put my hand over hers. "It's only one ancestor. I'll keep looking."

She nodded. "Thanks, Zoey."

I took my cue and got up to leave. "See you later."

I walked home and changed into sweatpants. Grabbed a soda from the fridge, then headed back to my office. I pulled a John Doe file out of my file cabinet and plopped down in my desk chair.

This case involved a man whose remains had been found in Central Michigan, about twenty years ago.

Wow. Talk about a cold case.

Foul play was suspected. I was just really digging in, when Karma came running into my office, meowing. I sighed and got up to follow her back down the hall. I saw Jason backing into my driveway. He got out and started to unfasten the cover over the bed of his truck.

He must have the boxes.

Between the two of us, it only took a few minutes to get the six boxes into the house and put them in a corner of my office. As he sat the last box down, he paused and looked at my murder board.

Damn it! I'd forgotten to turn it around to face the wall.

I sat on the floor and began to look through one of the boxes. I wasn't sure I'd find anything that would help with discovering more about the accused witches buried in the cemetery, but perhaps some light would be shed on the Rockman's, who, by all accounts, were a private family.

The first box was a gold mine. It contained a large, ornately covered family bible. I leafed through the delicate pages and saw that the blanks on the family tree page had all been filled in with neat handwriting. It went back four generations.

"Score!" I jumped to my feet.

"What?" Jason turned away from the murder board and came over to me.

"Look!" I handed him the bible.

After all, he was a Rockman and had every right to know any information about his family.

As he read, his eyes grew wide, and a smile slowly formed.

"This is amazing."

We both sank to the floor and sat side by side as we read all the names and dates. Extra pages had been added to accommodate all the children that were born to many of his family members.

"Can you help me piece this all together so it makes sense?" he said.

How could I say no? Genealogy was one of my passions. Not as much as collecting books, but it ran a close second.

"Of course." I fished into the box to pull out more papers.

"You think I should keep this and put it back into the house, or donate it to the historical society?" He shut the book.

I turned to look at him, and thought for a moment.

"Why don't we make copies of the genealogy pages and give them to the society? They don't need the entire bible. That way, it will stay in the family. Where it belongs."

"Perfect," he whispered, still staring in reverence at the bible. "You always know the right thing to do."

In that moment, I'd been given a glimpse of the old Jason, the one I'd fallen in love with.

We spent the rest of the afternoon sitting on the floor of my office, separating the papers in the boxes, into piles of birth certificates, death certificates, wills, and miscellaneous paperwork that would take a great deal of time to go through.

Jason left to pick up some burgers from Gil's, while I started to make files for all the information. On the inside of each file folder, I stapled a piece of notebook paper to make notes of what needed to be done with the contents of the file.

After we ate, Jason and I cleaned up my office, put the files in a few of the boxes, and sat them out of the way until I could get to them. I knew he wanted to stay and hang out, but I told him I was tired, in hopes that he would take the hint and leave.

As much as I enjoyed the time we'd spent together, I couldn't bring myself to trust him. Not just yet.

By the time Monday morning came around, I was chomping at the bit to get started. My first call was to Rodger Frost. I wanted to ask him about the police scene during the time Bea's relative was alive. I left him a voicemail telling him what I wanted, and gave him my phone number. I crossed my fingers that he would get back to me.

Since there was nothing more I could do on Bea's family until I heard from him, I went back to work on the John Doe case. There weren't that many matches in the database, and those that were there appeared to be distant relatives. This was going to take some time.

I opened my genealogy program and began to build a sketchy family tree. Most of the time, it's easier to work backward instead of forward. But this time it appeared I was starting somewhere in the middle. I entered all the data and decided to let the program do its thing and make connections for me.

Just as I closed out the program, my phone pinged. A text from Professor Frost. He said he had classes all week, but asked if we could meet over the weekend.

After pouring another cup of coffee, I went into my office to check my email. There was one regarding the files of Adrianna's parents. I could get them, but had to pay a copying fee. So I called the county and gave them my credit card number. The nice clerk offered to scan them and send them in an email. *Perfect!*

The anticipation was killing me, and it seemed to be taking forever to get the files. But within an hour, they showed up in my email. I eagerly read the pages as the printer spit them out. Adrianna's mother's file came through first. It was unremarkable, and the man who'd hit her was apprehended. He's been in prison for the last six months on a charge of armed robbery.

Well, that ended that. Her death truly had been just a tragic accident.

While I waited for Adrianna's father's file to print out, I went into the living room to open the blinds. As I did, I saw Jason looking out his front window, toward my house. So nothing had changed. I was hoping the Jason I saw the other night was back, and the possessive and controlling Jason had disappeared, but no such luck.

I heard the printer stop and grabbed the pages as I plopped down in my desk chair. There was a picture of the victim included in the documents, and for some reason he looked hauntingly familiar, like I'd seen him before, but I couldn't figure out where.

I shook my head. *Impossible.* He was dead when I was a little girl, and I'd never been to Paytonville. Adrianna said he disappeared when she was six, and we were about the same age.

According to the file, Tony Martinelli was last seen leaving a bar called the Stone Mill, in Paytonville, around midnight. His truck had been found a few miles away, in a ditch. It was on the route he would have taken to go home, but there was no sight of him. His keys and other personal items were still in the truck.

Hmm.

I shuffled through the pages and found photographs of the items found in his truck. In one of the pictures, his wallet was laying open and his driver's license, credit cards, and cash were displayed. So robbery wasn't the motive. Other pictures showed his keys, receipts for gas, and other items that shed little light on why or how he just disappeared off the face of the earth.

I read the official missing person report Adrianna's mother, Lauren, filed with the Paytonville Police Department. She'd last seen her husband when he'd left for work that morning. He'd been a mechanic at the car dealership in town. She told the police they weren't having money or marital problems—but who's going to admit that.

The police report noted that Lauren seemed to be highly anxious and distressed by the disappearance of her husband. Okay, that seemed normal. I can imagine being upset if someone I loved disappeared.

At the time of his disappearance, they checked his bank records and credit. Lauren had been telling the truth. They seemed to be in decent financial shape, and not behind with their bills. Maybe the witness interviews would give me more information.

The police interviewed his boss, who'd told them that Tony was a good worker who rarely called in sick. He had noticed that in the two weeks before his disappearance, Tony seemed to be upset and agitated about something, but wouldn't talk about it. His work performance didn't suffer, but he seemed guarded.

Hmm.

His co-worker's statements all repeated what this boss had said—that Tony appeared to be worried about something. One of his co-workers described him as being paranoid.

Now that's interesting.

The police also interviewed people who'd seen him at the bar the night he disappeared. They said it was normal for him to go to the bar after work on Friday's for a few drinks. One of the men echoed the feelings of Tony's co-workers about his change in behavior. The witness went on to say that the Friday night Tony disappeared, he was acting differently. Agitated, jumpy, like something had him spooked.

"What was going on with you, Mister Martinelli?" I sat back in my chair.

I read the rest of the file, but there was nothing to indicate why his behavior changed in the weeks leading up to his disappearance.

I set the papers aside and decided to check if anything popped up on the John Doe case I'd been working on. After all, I was paid to solve *those* cases, not the murder of those two girls.

There were a few hints, and as I went through them, my John Doe's family tree began to sprout. Now I just had to work on the different branches and see if any led to my mystery man. I opened the file and went back through it to see if there was something I had missed. When I'd started working on it, I had only looked at the DNA case number and the summary of his case. I'd only skimmed the rest of the paperwork.

One by one, I went through the pages. The last page was a composite sketch of what the victim may have looked like.

I gasped. *It couldn't be!*

I picked up the file on Adrianna's father and hurried to find his picture. They were the same person. Oh, my God! My John Doe was Adrianna's father.

I sat back in my desk chair, speechless. My hands were trembling, and I felt a shot of adrenaline shoot through my body like a rocket.

Calm down. You have to prove it. I took a few deep breaths to regain control.

There were a few things I had to do first.

I re-read the file on Tony Martinelli. Foul play was suspected. The Coroner had ruled the case a homicide due to the knife marks found on his bones, specifically his breastbone and ribs.

I needed the coroner's report.

I texted Agent Phillips, told him what I needed, and gave him the DNA and FBI file numbers. I told him it was urgent. He texted back and said he'd check and get back to me shortly.

While I waited, I paced around my office. Karma, who'd been sitting on my desk, watched me with her golden eyes. Evidently, I was not amusing enough for her taste, and she settled down on her blanket and commenced one of her long grooming sessions.

Even though only fifteen minutes had passed since I'd contacted Agent Phillips, it seemed like hours.

Finally, my phone pinged. Agent Phillips told me that Mabel would have a package for me in an hour. *Perfect!*

I was too wound up to work, and it was too early to leave to retrieve the package from Mabel's grave, so I used my nervous energy to clean out my refrigerator and make a grocery list. Karma needed cat food, and my cupboards were looking pretty bare.

I made it to the cemetery with ten minutes to spare, so I parked in my usual spot and waited for Agent Phillips. I leaned back against the headrest and closed my eyes. If I was right, how the hell was I going to tell Adrianna that her father has been found and that he'd been murdered.

Wait, that's not my job. The police could do that. *Whew!*

I opened my eyes just in time to see Agent Phillips's SUV pulling into the cemetery gates. He motioned for me to follow him.

That was strange. *We never talk to each other here.*

I started my Jeep and followed his vehicle around the perimeter of the cemetery. He cut up the road that ran through the center of the grounds, and pulled in behind the white caretaker's building. I pulled in next to him. Good spot. From the road, no one would know we were parked there.

He reached over and opened the passenger door to his black SUV. I got out of my truck and jumped into his.

"So what's going on?" He handed me a sealed manila envelope.

I told him about Adrianna's father disappearing when she was young, and that, according to the pictures, the John Doe was Tony Martinelli.

"Wow." He ran his hand over his hair. "Can you prove it?"

"I'm close. Mister Martinelli's daughter is an acquaintance of mine, and I just have to be sure. You know?" I hugged the envelope against my chest.

His eyes softened when he looked at me.

"I understand. This is what makes you good at what you do."

"Thanks." I reached for the door.

"Stay safe, Zoey." He put his hand on my shoulder.

"I will." I got out of the truck.

"I mean it. Keep your head down."

He put his SUV into gear and pulled away, leaving me standing there with my mouth hanging open.

What the hell was that about? Ugh. He's always so mysterious and full of intrigue. I wish he'd quit talking in code and just say what he has to say.

I yanked open the door to my Jeep and headed to the grocery store. As much as I just wanted to go home and look at the report, Karma liked to eat, and so did I.

The grocery store was busy, and it was taking longer than I'd expected to wind through the aisles. As I turned down the international food aisle, I saw Adrianna talking to a man I didn't recognize. They seemed to be pretty buddy-buddy, and didn't notice me.

Now what? Maybe she's dating someone, or they bumped into each other at the market.

After all, some people say the grocery store is among the best places to meet men. Never worked for me, but that doesn't mean anything.

I can't believe she would have any one she didn't know well in her life right now, given what's going on. He could be the killer, for God's sake.

I slipped my cell phone out of my bag to take a picture, but they both turned around to head down the next aisle. I backed up my cart and headed one aisle over. I was just in time to see them in the center of the aisle, and snapped a picture.

As much as I would have loved to be introduced to the mystery man, I didn't have the heart to face Adrianna, knowing her father's remains had been found, and the frozen food aisle wasn't the place to disclose that information. I turned around and went down another aisle to finish my shopping.

When I got to the checkout, Adrianna spotted me and waved. I waved back and prayed she wouldn't come and talk to me. But she did. The man she'd been with was nowhere to be seen.

We exchanged greetings, and she appeared to be in a great mood, which struck me as strange. I mean, if I were being targeted by a deranged killer, I sure as hell wouldn't be smiling and laughing.

"I saw you earlier," I said. "You were with some guy, and I didn't want to interrupt you."

"Oh, you should have! I would have introduced you to my brother, Tony."

I started to unload my groceries onto the conveyer belt.

"Your brother?"

"Yes. He's in town on business for a couple days." She maneuvered her cart into the lane next to mine.

"How fun. Sorry I didn't get to meet him. Talk later."

I felt horrible. *I'm such a bad friend. If she says she has a brother, even though she's never mentioned him before, that should be enough for me.*

While I was putting the groceries away, I paused long enough to pull up the picture I'd taken at the store, of Adrianna and her supposed brother. There wasn't any family resemblance. While Adrianna had dark hair and olive skin, the man was blond and had lighter skin. He could have been adopted.

It's none of your business. You're too suspicious. This is exactly why you don't have close friendships. Leave it alone.

Who was I kidding? As soon as I finished up with the groceries, I raced into my office. She'd said his name was Tony, named after his father, which would make him a junior.

I ran a search through every database I could, and there wasn't any record of Adrianna's mother giving birth to a son. In fact, in her mother's obituary, it stated she only had one child— Adrianna.

Why had she lied to me? *Damn it!* I knew it didn't feel right. *One day, I'm going to sit down with Adrianna and give her a piece of my mind.*

The coroner's report regarding Adrianna's father was on my desk, and I ripped open the envelope and found that he'd included a copy of the complete file the FBI had on this case. Elated, I sat back to read the information.

There were signs of defensive wounds on the forearm bones, and the coroner had ruled the death a homicide, and determined he'd bled to death due to his throat being cut.

Well, duh.

The coroner went into excruciating detail regarding the wounds, which was his job, but it was such a gruesome read it caused me to shiver.

I put the report aside, sat back in my chair, and closed my eyes to digest all the information.

An idea struck me, and I sat up and texted Nate.

Do you have a copy of the autopsy reports for the murdered women?

Yes, why?

Can you bring them over? It's important.

On the way.

While I waited for Nate, I went back through the case file for Adrianna's father. Forensics had been able to determine what kind of knife had been used, and had even included a picture of a knife that would be an example of the murder weapon.

How convenient.

Karma got up and stretched before leaping off my desk and racing down the hallway. Nate must have arrived.

I followed her, and when I got to the front door, Nate was just coming up the porch steps.

"Okay, so what's going on?" he said.

As we walked back to my office, I told him about the John Doe from the FBI turning out to be Adrianna's father, and the murder weapon that forensics believed to have caused his injuries.

He slid the other chair up to my desk, and pulled the murder books of the women out of his bag.

"Wow. What are the odds? So you're thinking it's the same murderer?" He gave me an incredulous look.

"I know it's a long shot, but we need to make sure, you know? The injuries sounded similar between the women and Adrianna's father."

I picked up Sienna's file and browsed through the labeled sections until I found the one I was looking for. Nate did the same with Natalie's murder book. We sat in silence, reading the reports and comparing their wounds to that of Adrianna's father.

Two hours later, we closed the murder books and put them on my desk. Nate stood and stretched. I sat back in my chair rubbed my eyes.

"What do you think? I looked up at him.

It's not so much the wounds." He sat back down. "It's the knife. According to all the reports, they seem to be the same type of weapon."

We both sat quietly and absorbed the implications of what it meant.

I got up and started to pace around the office—I always think better when I pace.

"But how is that possible?" I said.

Nate turned around in his chair and watched me pace.

"I mean, according to the FBI file, Adrianna's father died over twenty years ago. That would mean the killer would be well into his forties, if not his early fifties. I'm sorry, but Sienna and Natalie's murders don't seem to be the work of a man that age."

Nate shook his head and leaned back in his chair, his eyes closed.

"Maybe. But it's still not out of the realm of possibility."

He was right, but it still didn't make sense.

"But if we're working with the theory that Adrianna and the other two women are being targeted through a dating site," I said, "then the age the murderer would be now blows that theory out of the water. None of the women were even remotely interested in a middle-aged man, right? And it takes Chad Eastwick completely out of the picture as well."

"Right. None of their profiles indicated they'd been in touch with any man over thirty-five. Which means we're back to square one." Nate threw up his hands and got out of his chair, then walked over and stared at my murder board. "What are we missing?" He turned around and looked at me.

I stopped pacing and moved up beside him. "I don't know. It's possible that some of the men on the dating site lied about their age. People do it all the time. What do we do now?"

He picked up Natalie's murder book and handed it to me.

"We start over." He settled back into his chair, holding Sienna's book.

Two hours later, we weren't any further along, and we were both frustrated.

He closed Sienna's murder book and tossed it onto my desk. It landed with a *thud!* that caused me to jump.

"This is getting us nowhere. I'm hungry. Let's go get some dinner." He got up out of his chair and took Natalie's murder book out of my hands.

He put it with Sienna's, picked them both up, and walked out of the office. I glanced at the clock and saw it was almost seven. Where had the day gone?

I got up and headed down the hallway. Nate was standing in the middle of the living room, staring out the front window.

"Give me a minute to freshen up," I said, on my way to the bedroom.

He nodded, but didn't turn around.

At least he wasn't losing his cool and having a childish temper tantrum, like Jason would do. Besides, he definitely got brownie points for letting me see the murder books. I hoped he wouldn't get into trouble. He had probably broken a dozen regulations.

But who the hell was the murderer? We couldn't both be that wrong, could we?

Obviously, we could.

I sighed as I zipped up my boots and headed into the bathroom to brush my hair and teeth. I would have to contact Agent Phillips to see who was going to notify Adrianna. If the cases were connected, whose jurisdiction would that be?

I paused with my toothbrush poised in mid-air as I contemplated that nightmare.

"Are you ready?" Nate called from the living room.

I hurriedly ran a brush through my hair and pulled it back into a ponytail before joining him in the living room. He helped me into my coat, and we locked up the house before leaving.

He turned north, out of town.

"Where are we going?"

"I thought we'd go someplace different. Maybe getting out of our routine will shake things up a bit."

"Couldn't hurt." I settled back into the seat of his pickup truck.

We drove up the coast of Lake St. Clair, and along the St. Clair river. He pulled into one of the nicer restaurants just north of Algonac. I remembered this place. Jason and I once had dinner here.

We made a promise to not talk of murder over dinner, and we ended up having a fun evening. We traded stories about our lives, talked about our future dreams. His wants were simple. A nice house, a couple of kids maybe, and to continue being a detective. He loved small-town life and didn't want to transfer to a big city.

It was late by the time he dropped me off at home, and I fell into bed, exhausted. My dreams were filled with grotesque autopsy photographs and mangled skeletons. I forced myself to wake up a few times to get the images to stop, but it didn't work.

Peachy.

In the morning, I had a text from Nate, saying he'd talked to Agent Phillips, and that they were figuring things out.

Whew! That saved me a lot of worrying. But I wondered who was going to tell Adrianna about her father.

Speaking of Adrianna, who was that mystery man she was with at the grocery store? It certainly wasn't her brother. Man, she had to be one of the most frustrating people I'd ever met in my life. Except for my mother, of course.

While I waited for the coffee to brew, I checked my phone and saw a text from Agent Phillips, asking me to hang on to Tony Martinelli's file for a bit, until he and Nate figured everything out.

Made sense. They'd also have to get the Paytonville Police Department involved, because that's where the body was found.

What a mess! Glad it isn't my problem.

As hard as I tried to settle down and get some work done, I couldn't get the case out of my head. Nothing was making sense now, and it was driving me crazy. I sat for a long time and stared at the murder board, trying to figure things out.

After an hour, I felt as if the walls were closing in on me, and I was feeling claustrophobic. I needed to get out of there for a while.

I threw on a coat and walked the two blocks to Gil's. They weren't too busy yet, as it was still early, and I didn't have any trouble finding a booth by the front window. I was so lost in thought, I almost jumped out of my skin when my cell phone rang.

"Hello?"

"Zoey. Oh, thank goodness you answered." It was Bea.

"What's wrong"

"I forgot today is the day the Mavens of Mayhem are going to the casino. Can you come over and let Atlas out a couple times, and give him dinner?"

"Of course. Have fun."

Thanks, dear."

I finished my breakfast and jogged home. I noticed Bea's car was already gone, so I retrieved the spare key from my house and went next door to get Atlas. He gave me an enthusiastic greeting, and once I'd gathered his bowls, treats, and a plastic bag of his food, he bounded out the front door and ran to my house.

When Karma saw him, she ran to the top of her cat tree and meowed in protest at the German Shepherd running around the house.

"Get over it." I scratched her between the ears.

As much as I tried to get some work done, Atlas kept running in and out of my office and chasing Karma. Clearly, Bea hadn't been giving him much exercise lately, and he had a ton of pent-up energy.

I put on some warmer clothes and hiking boots, grabbed my coat and Atlas's leash, and went out to my truck. He needed to run. Atlas willingly jumped into the passenger seat, and as we drove out of town, I turned the heat on full blast and opened the window so Atlas could hang his head out. My problem now was where to go. I didn't want to take him to the woods by the witch cemetery, because I didn't want to run into Jason. Then I remembered there was a big park with trails that led through the woods in Clayton Township, about six miles away. It was kind of in the middle of nowhere, but it worked. I changed course and headed in that direction.

We pulled into a small parking area, and when I let Atlas out of the truck, he bounded into the open field. I stopped to read the historical plague. This park was used by missionaries as a settlement in the late 1700s. Then abandoned. Later, it was part of an attempt to build a canal from Lake St. Clair to the other side of the state. But it, too, failed. According to the sign, there were still foundations of old buildings and remnants of the canal building attempt.

Interesting.

I looked up and saw that Atlas had treed a squirrel and was circling the tree and whining.

"Come on, boy!"

Reluctantly, he gave up on the squirrel and ran over to me. The trees were just starting to bud, and the grass beginning to green up. The fresh smell of spring was in the air as Atlas and I ventured down one of the trails into the woods. He raced back and forth on the trail, his nose to the ground as he searched for a scent to follow. I thrust my hands in my coat pockets and followed him down the dirt path at a slower pace so I could absorb the scenery and enjoy the clean scent of the water flowing down the river, the birds announcing the arrival of spring, and the earthy, musky scent of the woods. The tension left my shoulders, and my body relaxed in the serene surroundings.

Atlas stopped and seemed to concentrate his nose on a particular patch of ground. Then he raised his head into the air and let out a howl that sent shivers racing up and down my spine. I started toward him, but before I reached him, he took off down the trail. His nose was on the ground, and his tail stood soldier straight, like an antenna. And the chase was on. I broke into a trot just too keep him in sight, but he sped up, and before I knew it I was sprinting. Still, I was losing ground, and soon lost sight of him.

I started to panic. Bea would kill me if I lost him.

I stopped to catch my breath. "Atlas!"

A bark rang out ahead of me and to the right, and he started to yip I sprinted down the path toward his yapping. The narrow path lined with trees on one side, and a large stone wall on the other soon gave way to a clearing. I could see cement and old roads.

I stopped. Rebar and other rubble littered the area, and with my luck, I'd fall and break something.

It was eerie walking through the deserted town. The birds had fallen silent, and there weren't any traces of squirrels, chipmunks, or even a spider web.

"A dead zone," I whispered. "But why?"

The only sound, other than my footfalls on the crushed stone and gravel, was that of Atlas. But even his yapping had turned to a whine, barely audible over the wind blowing through the trees.

I stopped and put my hands on my hips. "Atlas, where are you?"

He barked and started to whine again. As fast as I dared, I bolted through the town and toward him. I came out on what looked like an old dirt road. Looked to my left and saw the road ended at the woods, about a quarter-mile down. When I looked to my right, I saw Atlas walking around a partially burned-out delivery van, and past that, the orange and white fences which indicated a road was closed.

What the hell? What's that doing out here? And more importantly, is there anyone in it?

I should have brought my Uncle Felix's gun, but didn't think I'd need a weapon just to take a dog for a walk. Plus, even though I was becoming a good shot, I still wasn't over my fear of firearms.

I saw Atlas sit near the back of the van and whine. Experience had taught me that was his way of telling me there either was or had been a cadaver in or around the van.

Damn it! Now what do I do?

I reached into my coat pocket for my cell phone, but all I found were the keys to my truck. I'd left my phone in my bag—which was locked in my truck—over a mile away.

Peachy.

Just standing there wasn't doing me any good, so I walked over to the van and put Atlas on his leash.

"Good boy." I patted his head.

I started to creep around the vehicle. The back doors were shut, but I peered through the back window. Laying on the floor in back of the van was a partially scorched mattress. Metal shelves lined both sides of the van, but they appeared to be empty.

As I stood staring into the back of the van, Atlas started to whine and paw at the back door.

"It's okay, boy." I led him up the opposite side of the van, toward the driver's compartment.

The sliding door on the passenger side was open, and when I looked inside, I saw that the driver's compartment appeared to be much more charred than the back of the van. I didn't want to venture inside, because I wasn't sure what I was dealing with. Judging by all the cop shows I've seen, if there's a burned-out vehicle, it generally means that someone was trying to destroy something. Generally, evidence.

Come on, Atlas." I trotted back through the woods, to my truck.

I unlocked the door and grabbed my cell phone out of the bag. Nate answered on the second ring.

"Good morning! I had a great time—

"Me, too. Listen!"

I was met with silence, but I could hear him breathing through the phone.

I told him about the van and where I was.

"Okay, so why the excitement? Burned vehicles are found all the time."

Man, he was beginning to frustrate me.

"Atlas is with me. He was trained as a cadaver dog. He alerted toward the rear of the van. If he says there was a dead body in that van at one time, you can take it to the bank."

"Good enough for me. How do I get to the van? What road is it?"

"I don't know. It's closed. You might have to meet me in the parking lot and walk back with me."

"I've got a better idea. Why don't you go back to the van and mark it with your GPS and text me the coordinates? I'll start heading in your direction.

I hung up, and Atlas and I took off down the path to go over the uneven ground and tree roots that crisscrossed it. When we got back to the road, I used my GPS to get the coordinates, and sent them to Nate. I told Atlas to stay, and strode over to the van. Took out my cell phone and took as many pictures as I could of what I thought was important.

When I'd finished, I sat on the side of the road with Atlas, who was panting. Dark clouds rolled across the sky and blocked the sun, causing the woods to become dark and ominous. A heaviness hung in the air that wasn't there before. I had to stop this. I was starting to creep myself out.

"Come on. Let's get a drink." I got up and led Atlas back into the woods and down to the river.

We scrambled down a small embankment to a flat piece of concrete—a remnant of the canal building attempt. He put his head down and lapped up enough water to fill a camel. We returned to the road just in time to see Nate moving the *Road Closed* sign off to the side to allow the police personnel down the road. His truck, a police car, and a crime scene unit drove down the road and stopped a short distance from the van. I got up and went to join him.

Atlas, who usually gives everyone an enthusiastic greeting, walked up and nudged Nate's hand with his nose before laying down at my feet. He put his head down on his front paws and sighed.

"This is going to take hours." Nate kept his gaze on the van. "Why don't you go home, and I'll call you later?"

As much as I wanted to stay to see what they found, I knew he was right. There wasn't any point in me staying.

I nodded, and Nate gave me a quick kiss goodbye, then signaled to one of the policemen who was standing by his patrol car.

"Can you take her back to her car?

Grateful for the ride, Atlas and I piled into the back of the police car, and within a minute or two, found ourselves back at my vehicle. When we got home, I disappeared into my office, and Atlas joined me. He plopped down on the rug in front of the murder board, and sighed. Within a minute, he was fast asleep, sending cute doggy snoring sounds wafting through the house. I was jealous. I would have loved a nap.

I retrieved my cell phone from my bag, plugged it into my computer, and uploaded the pictures of the van. I studied each one, but the problem was I didn't know what I was looking for. Frustrated, I saved them to a folder and decided to work on one of the FBI files. For a change of pace, I pulled out a file from the Wanted Criminals drawer. The unidentified human remains were important, but if I could find out who one of the criminals were, maybe I could prevent them from committing more crimes.

The first file I pulled out was of a pedophile and murderer. *Ugh!* I read through it, and the details made my stomach churn. To make matters worse, his DNA had been found on three dead children so far, but he wasn't in the system. I had to put the file down to fight off the wave of nausea that pulsed through my body. Maybe I wasn't cut out for this type of work. I had to develop a thicker skin. This work was important.

Just as I logged into the DNA program, my cell phone pinged. A message from Agent Phillips.

Just left Adrianna's house. She could use a friend. Told her about her dad.

Let her call a friend, if she has one left. I was so frustrated with her I could have cared less if she was upset.

I'm sorry, what? he replied.

Then the guilt set in. *Thanks, Mom.*

I sighed, and typed, *Never mind. I'm on the way.*

That's the response I wanted.

I could almost hear his voice chastising me, and I wrinkled my nose up at the phone before tossing it onto my desk.

"Come on, Atlas." I sighed again.

We pulled into Adrianna's driveway five minutes later, and I had to force myself to get out of the truck. As I walked up her driveway, I noticed her car was gone.

What the hell? I rang the doorbell and knocked, but it was obvious she wasn't home.

I got back into my truck and texted Agent Phillips.

She's not home. I tried.

Thanks.

My head told me I should probably go look for her, but I wouldn't have any idea where to start, and my heart just wasn't in it, so I drove back home.

As I worked on the FBI unknown sub, as they called it, the burned-out delivery van kept creeping into my thoughts. *Why hasn't Nate called me yet?*

I picked up my phone to call him, but thought better of it. He was probably busy. He'd call when he had time.

Atlas got up and stretched, and I did the same. After I had let him out, I gave Karma and him their dinner. It was almost dinner time for me as well. I opened the fridge and freezer, but didn't see anything I wanted to make, so I decided to order in. I riffled through the junk drawer in the kitchen and found the menus for the restaurants in town that delivered. I had just picked up the phone to order when it rang, causing me to jump. It was Nate.

"Hey, want Chinese food?" I said.

"Perfect. I'll pick it up on my way to your place."

He gave me his order, and showed up fifteen minutes later.

"Preliminary tests show that some of the blood we found in the van matches Natalie's," he said, as we settled down to dinner, "and the van that turned up in the same condition a couple weeks ago had traces of Sienna's blood in it."

My heart sank. "That's sad. So he's killing them in the delivery van?"

"Looks that way."

Something in my brain clicked. I closed my eyes and replayed the morning of Sienna's murder in my head. On my morning run, I'd gone to the park and crossed the road at Main Street.

I opened my eyes and sat straight up in my chair.

"I've got it!"

Nate looked at me.

"The morning Sienna's body was discovered, I remember seeing a van just like the burned-out one when I crossed the street from the park. The driver stopped and let me cross."

Nate set his chopsticks down on the plate. "Okay, but this company's delivery vans are everywhere. The odds of it being the same one…"

"True. But how many of those vans are out at 6:00 a.m.?"

He raised an eyebrow. "The drivers don't start until eight. Did you get a look at the driver?" He sat forward in his chair.

I paused to think back. "No. He had his head down and was wearing a hat."

"What kind of hat?"

"It was one of those flat types with the bill in front. I don't know what it's called." I shrugged.

"A flat cap. It's called a flat cap."

I gave him a sideways glance. "If you say so."

After we finished dinner, he got a call and had to leave. He gave me a kiss goodbye and disappeared into the night. I checked my phone and saw I'd missed a call from Bea. Her message said the Mavens of Mayhem were having such a good time they'd decided to spend the weekend, and could I take care of Atlas for a few days. I tried to call her back, but it went straight to voicemail. I told her to have fun, and that Atlas and I would hang out.

It was getting late, and I knew I should go to bed, but I was restless. The activities of the day had me wired, and I knew it would be impossible to shut off my brain.

I put on a pair of tennis shoes, leashed up Atlas, and headed out the front door. Perhaps a walk would calm me enough to get some much-needed sleep.

We walked through the park down to the beach. I let Atlas off his leash to chase the gentle waves that were licking at the shore. It didn't dawn on me until he was already soaked to the skin that I'd be sharing my bed with a wet dog. *Peachy.*

After his swim, we strolled through town and down one of the side streets. Within a few minutes, I found myself standing in front of Adrianna's house. The lights were on in her living room, and the curtains open just enough for someone to be able to see what was going on inside the house.

Adrianna was standing in the middle of the room, and it looked like she was talking to someone who was just out of sight. I pulled Atlas closer to me and walked over to a large oak tree in front of her house. I tried to blend in with the massive tree trunk. Plus, it offered me a better vantage point.

As I watched, Adrianna moved farther into the room, and the person she'd been talking to moved toward her.

Jason! What the hell?

Must have something to do with her father's murder.

I couldn't think of any other reason he'd be at her house. I didn't want to stick around and get caught snooping—especially by Jason.

As Atlas and I walked home, I had conflicting feelings about seeing Jason with another woman, even if it was an innocent encounter. On one hand, I'd be happy because maybe he would leave me alone. But on the other hand, I couldn't help but feel a tad jealous.

As nice as Nate was, he was kind of a Boy Scout. While Jason had that whole bad boy vibe going on. Which, as much as I hated to admit it, was really attractive.

Jason's truck passed me and disappeared down our street. When I got home, I found him waiting for me on my porch. He stood as I came up the stairs, and as we approached him, all the hair on Atlas's back stood on end, and I felt his body tense up next to me.

"It's okay, boy," I whispered.

I unlocked the door and let Atlas run ahead of us. I gave him a bowl of water, and Jason pulled two beers out of the fridge and sat at the kitchen island.

"What's up?" I sipped my beer.

I was exhausted and in no mood for an argument.

"I just left Adrianna's house." He put his head down. "She's pretty broken up about her dad."

"Why were you there? Agent Phillips did the notification."

He looked up at me, narrowed his eyes and set his jaw.

"How do you know?"

I told him about Agent Phillips texting me about going over there.

"She wasn't home when I got there. She must have left right after he did."

"Where did she go?"

I don't know." I shrugged. "It's not my day to babysit her. But you still didn't answer my question."

"She called me and asked me to come over. I think she just needed someone to talk to."

"And she chose you?" I raised an eyebrow.

He laughed. "Yeah, caught me by surprise, too." He drained his beer and got up from the bar stool to put his bottle in the sink. "I heard you found the van. Look, I know I've been a real jerk lately, but there's something you need to understand."

"I'm listening."

"There's something going on. I can't tell you about it, but it has the potential to put you in very serious danger. I don't know what I'd do if something happened to you."

For a second, I thought I saw a tear in his eye, which he quickly wiped away with the back of his hand.

"Like what?" I said.

That he was so concerned made me feel uneasy.

"It's FBI stuff. Nothing that involves you directly. You're just going to have to trust me on this, Zoey. Lay low, please."

I went to the front door and opened it for him. "I'll see what I can do."

He shot me a dirty look before leaving. I slammed it behind him.

Is he resorting to the threat of danger to try to keep me in line? That's the new tactic? I don't think so.

I locked the doors, turned out the lights, and went to bed.

I woke up late and had to scramble to get ready in time to meet the professor, but managed to make it out the door with a couple minutes to spare. When I arrived at Gil's, Professor Frost was waiting for me on the sidewalk.

"Good morning, Miss Callaway." He opened the restaurant door for me.

"Good morning, Professor. Thank you. And please, call me Zoey."

We found a booth near the back where it was quieter, and ordered coffee.

"Did you run into a problem on Bea's genealogy?" he said.

"Yes and no." I furrowed my brow and took the folder with Bea's information out of my messenger bag, and handed it to him. "I can't figure out why a chief inspector in the London area would be walking the beat, but I'm not that familiar with the British police culture during that period."

"Now why are on earth are you interested in a London chief inspector?" He looked at me quizzically.

"He arrested Bea's ancestor. It's all in there." I pointed to the file.

The professor sipped his coffee as he looked over the information. I added cream and sugar to my cup and waited patiently for him to digest everything.

"Martinelli…of course!" He laughed. "Apparently, he was well-known—should I say, infamous. He used his power to pick up these poor girls. He earned the awful nickname, the Inspector of Prostitutes. It seems likely that Bea's poor relative was one of those girls." Rodger giggled. "He helped."

"Oh, my gosh." I laid my fork down on my plate, shoulders slumped. "Oh, Bea's not going to like this. She's not going to like this one bit." I sighed.

"Yes, it's not something one likes to find out about one's ancestors. But remember, my dear, it was a different time. She was a widow with children. She had to make a living any way she could. Quite noble, in a way."

"Perhaps." I shrugged. "But Bea's not going to see it that way."

"Unfortunate. Would you like me to talk to her for you?"

"No, but thanks." I reached to pick up the file and put it back into my bag.

As I went to close the folder, it hit me—*Inspector Martinelli. No, it couldn't be.*

The shock must have registered on my face, because the professor gave me a concerned look.

"Is there something wrong, Zoey?"

"No. It's just that the chief Inspector has the same last name as an acquaintance of mine."

How did I miss that the first time? It has to be a coincidence. After all, there must be a million Martinellis, and Adrianna's family is from Italy, not Britain.

"Oh?" he said. "Who?"

"There's a young woman in town, named Adrianna Martinelli. She's been having a bit of trouble lately, and I've been trying to help her."

"Really?" He paused for a minute. "No, I don't I think I know her. Any way I can help?"

"That's sweet of you. But I don't think her problem is in your line of expertise, Professor."

"Perhaps. But maybe I can."

He had a point. And it would be nice to tell him what was going on, and see if he had a fresh perspective, because quite frankly, I was stumped.

While we finished our breakfast, I gave him the short version of the recent murders, and how notes were found directed at Adrianna, without giving away the content of those notes.

He listened intently, and when I'd finished, he pushed his plate away and signaled to the waitress to bring us more coffee.

"That is quite a tale," he said. "And the poor girl has no idea who is doing this?"

"She says she doesn't." I shrugged.

"But…?"

"But she has a habit of telling half-truths, or leaving out important information."

"Ahh. Lying by omission.

"Exactly."

"Makes you wonder if she's involved somehow, doesn't it?" He sat back in his seat and put a finger to his lips.

"It does. But I think she's just scared."

"And you're working with the police on this matter?"

"Not really. My uncle was a sheriff. Before he died, we would try and solve cold cases. I just love a good mystery. Plus, I was out jogging when I heard Adrianna scream and ran to her house the morning the first body was found on her porch."

"How dreadful for you!"

I nodded. "Thanks. It wasn't a pretty sight."

"I can imagine. I'm so sorry you had to go through that." He grabbed the check the waitress had left on the table. "This one's on me. I hate to break up our delightful meeting, but I have a stack of essays to grade."

"Thank you for meeting with me, Professor." I stood.

He helped me into my coat. "The pleasure was all mine." He shook my hand, and went to the register to pay the bill.

We parted on the sidewalk, and I took my time walking home. Maybe I could delay telling Bea anything until I had more information. I still had work to do on the unsub for the FBI, and that paid the bills.

I pulled up the genealogy website and was pleased to find a number of hints waiting for me. *This may not take as long as I thought it would.*

Three hours later, I was very close to identifying the horrid man that had abused those children, but just needed one more connection. I took a break to let out the dog and stretch my legs. While I was waiting for Atlas to finish his business, I saw a moving van back into the house next door. Abbey had lived there up until a few months ago, and the house had been vacant ever since. The owner had listed it for sale right after Abbey had moved out. It must have sold.

Where have I been? It would be nice to have a new neighbor.

I knelt on the sectional and gazed out the front window, trying to catch a glimpse of the new owners. A black SUV pulled up and parked on the street, followed closely by a gray pickup truck. A woman about my age got out of the SUV. Her blonde hair was pulled back into a short ponytail. Her navy blue sweatsuit revealed that she was chunky, but not obese. She stood on the sidewalk and looked at the pickup truck. Must have been waiting for her husband.

He turned out to be a big guy. Not fat, but tall and stocky. Clean cut, with short dark hair. Maybe military. There was a base only a few miles away.

They embraced and kissed. I smiled and turned away. *How exciting for them to have a new house.*

Atlas was barking at the back door, so I let him in and gave him a treat before getting back to work. Another solid two hours of work paid off.

"Gotcha!" I squealed in delight.

I texted Agent Phillips that Mabel had a package.

He texted back, *One hour.*

Perfect. I printed out all the documentation and wrote a short report outlining my findings. Then I put them all in a manilla envelope and sealed it.

As much as I wanted to work on the murders, I was too giddy from my success at helping to get a monster off the streets to concentrate.

I took Atlas with me, and we got to the cemetery with ten minutes to spare. I parked close to Mabel's grave, and tucked the envelope into its usual spot. After I moved my Jeep a good distance away, I put Atlas on his leash and jogged a couple laps around the cemetery. He needed the exercise, and I needed to burn off some nervous energy.

As we rounded the curve at the back of the cemetery, I saw Agent Phillips's black SUV pull through the front gates. As he walked over to the gravesite, he glanced over at my truck, and a shocked look crossed his face when he realized it was empty. I saw him scan the cemetery, and his concerned look turned into a smile when he saw me with the dog.

The old oak trees temporarily blocked my view of him, and by the time I got back to my truck, Agent Phillips's SUV was just pulling out of the cemetery. I put Atlas in the car and pulled my cell phone out of my pants pocket. There was a text from Agent Phillips.

Stay in the shadows. Keep the dog.

"*Ugh!*" I stomped my foot and threw my phone onto the passenger seat.

I was so tired of him talking in riddles.

As I drove home, I realized that maybe I'd dismissed Agent Phillips's veiled warnings too easily, in light of what Jason said yesterday.

"It's so frustrating!" I said to Atlas, and banged my fist on the steering wheel.

He laid across the center console and put his head on my lap. I stroked his head the rest of the way to the house. When we pulled into the driveway, the new neighbor was outside, sweeping her front porch. Atlas bounded out of the car and ran toward her. His tail was up, and his tongue was hanging out of his mouth.

"Atlas!" I ran to intercept him.

I wasn't fast enough. He'd bounded up the porch steps and was greeting the new neighbor.

"I'm really sorry," I said, as I caught up to him.

"He's fine. I'm Shannon Davis." She held her hand out.

The gaze of her bright blue eyes met mine, and she smiled.

I shook her hand. "I'm Zoey. Welcome to the hood." I snapped Atlas's leash into place on his collar. "Sorry about that. I'm dog sitting for Bea, who lives on the other side of me."

Shannon knelt down and scratched Atlas's his ears. He moaned with pleasure.

"Do you want to come in for some coffee?"

"I'd love to, but I'm really busy this morning. How about if we plan on a glass of wine this afternoon?"

"Perfect." She stood and smiled.

"Great. Just pop over around two. Nice to meet you." I turned to leave.

After making sure Karma and Atlas had everything they needed, I retreated to my office to review the murder board. I was missing something, and come hell or high water, I had to figure it out.

I printed the pictures of the burned-out van and tacked them onto my murder board. It wasn't out of the realm of possibility that the person who'd killed Adrianna's father had also killed the two women, given that the wounds and knife were similar on all the victims. Granted, the only connection between Adrianna and the other women was the dating site, but that wasn't set in stone. As for the murder weapons, there had to be hundreds, if not thousands, of the same knife in the marketplace, so that wasn't going to help narrow things down either.

My gaze wandered back to the two men that all three women had talked to on the dating sites. Maybe...

I pulled up the dating site on my computer and cringed as I opened an account. I scoured my computer for a decent picture of myself, and uploaded it onto the site. I also uploaded a picture of Adrianna and myself that I found on my phone, but couldn't remember when we'd taken it.

Oh, snap! We'd taken a selfie after meeting for lunch one day. Since I'd offered myself up as bait, I figured it wouldn't hurt to make the connection between Adrianna and myself obvious. I just prayed Jason or Nate didn't see this.

After filling in my profile, which took a considerable amount of time, considering I was trying to use some of the same things as the two murder victims did on their profiles, I decided to hunt down my suspects.

It didn't take long to find Daniel Parchinelli and Peter Billings. Even though I didn't think Marcus had anything to do with this mess, I included him anyway. I gave them each a wave—or whatever it was called—and sat back to wait.

Within a few minutes, a private message popped up on my screen from Daniel Parchinelli. He said hi, and that he liked my profile. I told him I liked his as well, and we chatted for a bit. He was working at a job near Hope Harbor and wanted to know if I would meet him for lunch. I begged off, saying I couldn't get out of work, but asked him to breakfast in the morning, at Gil's. He agreed, and I signed out.

I did an hour's worth of work, but couldn't get my mind off the murders. I looked at the picture I'd taken in the grocery store, of Adrianna and her mystery man. If only Adrianna hadn't lied about who he was.

"That's it!" I sat straight up in my chair.

I had to find out who that guy was.

I grabbed my bag and drove over to Adrianna's. It wasn't until I pulled into her driveway that I remembered she'd be at work. *Damn it!* I'd have to come back later.

I decided to leave her a note telling her I wanted to talk to her, so I pulled a piece of paper out of the small notebook I kept in my bag, and scrawled a message on it. As I approached the front door, I saw a piece of paper sticking out from the edge of her doormat. It hadn't been there long, because the paper was still clean. I knew I should probably leave it alone, that it wasn't any of my business, but I couldn't resist.

I crouched down and picked up the note. Unfolded the paper and saw the same handwriting that'd been on the note safety-pinned to the murder victims.

It read: *I'm still here.*

I gasped and looked around to see if there was anything suspicious or out of place. Other than an elderly man walking his dog, the sidewalk was deserted. I dashed back to my truck and called Nate to tell him about the note. He told me to stay put.

A minute or two later, Nate pulled up and parked his truck on the street in front of Adrianna's house, then walked up to my driver's side window.

"Where's the note?"

I nodded toward the house. "On the porch. I picked it up. I'm sorry."

"You didn't know. It's okay. Go home. I'll take it from here."

I agreed and backed out of the driveway. It wasn't until I turned the corner onto my street that I realized a black car with tinted windows was behind me. It resembled the one Adrianna had described as following her. I didn't want to lead him to my front door, so I kept driving. The car matched me turn for turn, and I wasn't so much scared as I was pissed off. It would've been useless to try to outrun him, so I did the next best thing—led him to the police department. I grabbed the folder I'd taken to Adrianna's, and my cell phone, then walked into the police station. I turned around once I was in the vestibule, and saw the car take off. I rushed outside to try to get a picture of the license plate, but

I hadn't been quick enough. Before leaving the police station, I filed a report regarding the car and being followed.

It was almost two o'clock by the time I got home, and Shannon was due to come over in a few minutes. I opened a bottle of wine to let it breath, and got out a couple wine glasses. After my morning, a glass of wine was just what I needed. I opened the front door and made sure the storm door was shut properly so Atlas and Karma wouldn't escape. Then I poured a glass of wine and retreated to my office for another look at the murder board.

"Zoey?" I heard Shannon call out.

"Come in!" I headed to the front.

We exchanged greetings, and I poured her a glass of wine.

"Your house is so nice." She looked around the living room.

"Thanks. So what brings you to Hope Harbor?"

She told me that her husband was indeed in the military, as I'd suspected, and stationed at the base a few miles away. She was a librarian, and was hoping one of the libraries might be hiring.

We were chatting away like jaybirds, when Nate came strolling through the front door.

Damn. I'd forgotten to lock it.

"Why the hell didn't you call me and tell me you were being followed?" He glared at me and ran his hand through his hair. Then he saw I wasn't alone. "Oh, sorry. Hello. I'm Nate, a detective at the Hope Harbor Police Department."

Shannon and he exchanged greetings, and then he turned his attention back to me.

"Well?"

"I...you were busy with the note from the killer. I didn't want to bother you. Plus, I handled it."

I was shocked. Nate had never lost his temper with me before.

He opened his mouth to say something, but thought better of it and took a couple deep breaths instead.

"Okay, for now. I'll pick you up at six. This discussion isn't over." He turned to face Shannon. "Nice to meet you."

When he left, I looked at Shannon. "Sorry about that." I felt myself blush.

"What was that about?"

I sighed. "It would be easier to show you. Follow me." I got up and led her to my office.

For the next hour, I told her about the case and the various suspects—or lack of suspects. She listened intently, and when I'd finished, she got up from my desk chair and walked over to the murder board.

"Interesting," she said, when she got to the pictures of the burned-out delivery van.

"What?" I stood next to her.

She pointed to the picture of the burned-out driver's cab.

"Whoever did this was more interested in hiding their identity than concealing that a woman was murdered in the back of the van."

"Huh? How can you tell?" I looked at the picture again.

"See how much more damage has been done to the driver's compartment, and there's very little damage to the back of the van?" She pointed to the picture of the back of the van.

I studied both pictures with a new perspective.

"Yes, you're right. How did you spot that?" I looked at her.

"My father was an arson investigator for years. When I was growing up, sometimes on weekends I'd go with my dad to look at burned-out buildings and stuff." She smiled at a memory. "I just kind of learned by osmosis."

I put my arm around her shoulders and gave her a hug.

"You're amazing," I said.

We poured more wine and kept talking about the case. It was almost five o'clock before she left.

I was elated. I felt as if I'd met a kindred spirit. A partner in crime, so to speak.

Nate called me at 5:30 and said he had to beg off. He was with Adrianna, telling her about the note, and he expected to be working late into the night.

No problem. I wasn't in the mood to see him, anyway.

I made myself a tuna fish sandwich and ate dinner with Atlas and Karma before going back to my office to attempt to catch up on my real job. Today had been a wasted day as far as work was concerned.

By midnight, I'd made good progress on finding one of the people on the FBI's unsub list, and I was tired. I walked through the house, checking all the windows and doors. As I shut the front blinds, I saw a dark car that resembled the one that had followed me earlier, creeping down the street. Shivers ran up and down my spine as I watched it go past my house. I should've called Nate or Jason…but tell them what? It wasn't a crime to drive down a road.

After setting the house alarm, I curled up in bed with Atlas and Karma. Bea was due home tomorrow, and I had to admit I'd miss Atlas. Just his presence made me feel safer.

Atlas must have sensed my mood, because he army crawled further up the bed until his body was stretched out against mine, and he put his head on my pillow. I wrapped my arm around him and sighed. I slept like a baby, knowing he was watching over me.

20

I woke with a start sometime in the middle of the night. Atlas was standing at the end of my bed, growling. I lay perfectly still and strained my ears, trying to hear if anyone was moving around the house.

I had set the alarm. *What the hell?*

I didn't hear anything, but I eased out of bed, and slid open the nightstand drawer. I felt around until I touched the gun, and gripped it.

"Let's go, boy," I whispered, and grabbed Atlas's collar.

He jumped off the bed, and we ventured out of the bedroom, down the hallway toward the kitchen.

The alarm would have gone off, right? There couldn't be anyone here.

I flattened myself against the wall as I crept, with the gun at my side. Everything was quiet. Maybe he had heard something outside.

Simultaneously, I flipped on the hallway light, let go of Atlas's collar, and yelled, "Get him!"

Atlas burst into the living room, and I followed, my gun in front of me. I felt along the wall for the kitchen light switch, and flicked it on. The dog was standing on the back of the sectional and using his nose to lift one of the blinds so he could see outside. He was barking and growling.

Damn it! Someone had to be outside. *Where did I put my cell phone?*

I darted across the kitchen and living room, and ran down the hallway on the opposite side, toward my office. I found my cell phone on my desk and dialed Jason's number. I hated to do it, but he lived across the street, and Nate was a couple miles away.

"Hello," he answered, his voice thick with sleep.

"Atlas is going nuts," I whispered into the phone. "I think there's someone outside my house."

"Stay low."

The phone clicked as he hung up. I crawled down the hall and joined Atlas on the sectional. I made myself as small as possible before daring to peek outside, over the top of the couch. I saw Jason run out of his house, the silhouette of a gun in his hand. He kept low and stopped to duck behind his truck, which was parked in the street.

It was dangerous to do this by himself. *I should help.*

I ran down the hallway and slipped into a pair of sneakers before turning off the alarm and going to the back door. I turned on the floodlights and looked around. Nothing was moving. Maybe someone was in my garage, which was detached and sat on the property just past the back of the house.

I darted back into the kitchen and grabbed my cell phone. Opened the garage door app and strode outside. Held my gun out in front of me and hit the button on my phone to open the garage door. I heard it creak open and caught Jason out of the corner of my eye, coming down the driveway.

"Stay back!" he headed into the garage out of sight.

I held my breath until he reappeared. We stood in front of the garage, looking at each other.

"You're clear," he said.

I opened my mouth to say something, but a car started up somewhere close, and lit up their tires as they peeled out. Jason and I ran down the driveway to the street just in time to see the taillights of a car careen around the corner, toward town.

"You okay?" He tucked his gun into the pocket of his dark bathrobe.

"Fine. Sorry. Thanks."

I felt horrible. It'd obviously been a false alarm.

"Let's go inside." He took my hand and led me back into the house.

I shut and locked the back door. Atlas ran to greet us, and gave us both a good sniff to make sure we were still in one piece.

"You want me to stay?" Jason relaxed his shoulders.

"Don't be silly. I'm fine. Sorry I woke you up." I opened the front door to let him out.

The front porch light flicked on, and I saw a piece of paper sticking out from the corner of my welcome mat. Looked to be the same kind of paper the killer used.

I gasped. Jason followed my gaze and saw the paper.

"Get me some tweezers or something."

I retrieved my eyebrow tweezers from the bathroom and handed them to him. He reached down and picked up the paper, squeezing the tweezers.

"Call Nate."

I nodded and did what he said.

"Get back in the house and grab a plastic bag."

Sheesh. I was beginning to feel like an errand girl.

Jason followed me inside and shut the door. I grabbed a plastic ziplock bag from the pantry and opened it. Jason got a fork out of the drawer and opened the note before sliding it into the bag and zipping it shut.

The note had been written on the same card stock the killer had used. The ink looked the same, but the writing was different. It was in cursive, not calligraphy, and read: *Bad things happen to little girls who don't mind their own business.*

I clapped my hand over my mouth and collapsed onto one of the bar stools. Atlas's bark caused me to jump and yelp. Someone knocked at the door.

Jason let Nate in, and we explained what happened and showed him the note. Nate listened, read the note, and looked at me.

"Who did you piss off?"

I shrugged. "I don't know."

But in the back of my mind, I thought of the black sedan and my contact with Daniel Parchinelli. All of this had started after I'd made contact with him.

I shook my head. *Circumstantial.*

Maybe it had something to do with Agent Phillips's veiled warnings.

No. People who play in that sandbox wouldn't leave a note before they strike, would they?

The three of us chatted for a bit longer, before both men left. I locked the door behind them and set the alarm.

"Come on, Atlas."

We both climbed back into bed. Karma, who'd slept through most of it, gave me a withering look at having her beauty sleep disturbed, before settling back down.

I tossed and turned the rest of the night. I couldn't shut my head off, and every little noise caused me to tense up.

At 5:00 a.m., I abandoned all hopes of sleep, and got out of bed to let the dog out and feed him and Karma. While I waited for Atlas to come in, I started my coffee and brushed my teeth. I had to meet Daniel in a couple hours, and I didn't have the will go out for my morning run.

After the animals were taken care of, and the caffeine from the coffee was jump-starting my body, I went into my office to check my email. My cell phone alerted me to a text from Agent Phillips.

Heard you had some excitement last night. Maybe you should go out of town for a bit. Stay safe. If you need anything, text me 24/7.

How the hell did he find out what happened so fast? Jason, of course!

I texted Agent Phillips back and thanked him. But I was fine. I don't scare easily, and I don't tuck tail and run.

I got up and paced around my office. I was pissed at Jason for telling Agent Phillips about what had happened last night. First, it was none of his business. And second, Jason was now messing with my livelihood. Agent Phillips could think the work I was doing for him was too dangerous, and yank me off the job. I needed the salary I earned from the FBI to pay my bills.

I went into the kitchen to get more coffee, and saw Jason getting into his truck, across the street. I darted out the front door and tapped on the driver's side window. He rolled it down.

"Why did you tell Agent Phillips about what happened last night?" I crossed my arms over my chest.

He ran his hands through his hair. "This isn't a game, Zoey. Whether you want to believe it or not, you're in danger. The way I see it, you have two choices. You can either back off, or bury your head in the sand, like Adrianna, and hope it'll all go away."

My body started to tremble. Partially because it was cold outside and I was in my pajamas. But mostly because I was angry.

"Actually, I have three choices. My third choice is to find out who killed those girls and is terrorizing Adrianna. Which is exactly what I plan on doing."

I turned my back on him, stomped into the house, and slammed the door behind me.

Before I left to meet Daniel, I ran next door and filled Shannon in about what I was doing. She offered to go to Gil's and sit near us to make sure I was safe.

Perfect!

I walked into town and found a booth by the window. A few minutes later, a black sedan pulled into a parking spot in front of the restaurant. It resembled the one that had followed me, but I couldn't be sure. There were four other black sedans parked in town as well—I'd noticed them as I trekked toward Gil's.

A man I recognized as Daniel Parchinelli got out of the black car and looked around before he headed into the restaurant. I waved. He saw me and smiled. As he came toward me, his steel-toed work boots thumped on the wood floor.

He was more attractive in person. His blonde hair and blue eyes were accentuated by his high cheekbones. I admired his broad shoulders and narrow waist. His biceps were straining to escape from his red and white flannel shirt.

A man with big biceps—every woman's dream.

Stop it. Remember why you're here.

Those amazing biceps made it easy to overpower a woman. Not to mention, most men.

Shannon followed him into the restaurant and sat at a table a short distance away. She pretended to read, but I could see her watching us.

Like most blind dates, it was awkward, to say the least. We fumbled through conversation about what we did for a living, and our families. He was a project manager for a construction company, and had two younger brothers and a sister. His family wasn't close because his father was an alcoholic and could be abusive.

"I can relate." I took a sip of my coffee. "My mother is an alcoholic, and verbally abusive. I practically raised myself."

"I'm sorry to hear that. What about your dad?"

I swallowed the lump in my throat. "He committed suicide when I was seven. Guess he couldn't take it." I shrugged.

Pity and sympathy filled his eyes. I hated that. I didn't want people to feel sorry for me.

"That had to be tough," he said.

"It made me stronger. I learned to depend on no one but myself. You seem to have risen above your past as well."

"I have now. I got into trouble when I was younger. I was just so angry." His eyes flashed, but he quickly brought it under control. "I went to therapy and distanced myself from my family. It's helped."

At least he'd realized he needed help, and got it. He was falling off my suspect list, but not all the way.

"So did you ever go out with one of my friends, Adrianna Martinelli?" I said.

He looked up from his eggs, and his gaze met mine.

"Girl code, you know."

"Girl code?" He gave me a puzzled look.

Was he trying to buy time instead of answering my question?

"You know." I smiled. "If one of your girlfriends is going out with a guy, or has dated a guy, then he's hands-off."

"Seriously?" He chuckled.

"Hey, girl code is a thing, and it's serious." I stared into his eyes. "So did you date Adrianna?"

"Adrianna who?"

I could tell by the way his cheeks reddened he was lying. But I decided to play along. I pulled the picture of Adrianna and I up on my cell phone, and showed it to him.

"Oh, her. Yeah, we went out once. I'm not dating anyone, let alone her."

We chatted a few more minutes, before leaving. He scribbled his phone number on the back of one of the takeout menus from Gil's and handed it to me.

"I'd love to see you again," he said.

"Me, too." I touched his arm.

He had to get to work. We said goodbye outside, and he gave me a sweet kiss on the cheek. If he wasn't a murder suspect, I could fall for him in a heartbeat.

While I was walking home, my cell phone rang. It was Bea.

"Hi, hon! Just letting you know I'll be home this afternoon."

"No worries, Bea. I'm glad you're having fun. And I love having Atlas."

I could hear the noise of the casino in the background.

"Thanks, Zoey. Love you!"

I pulled the menu out of my coat pocket and looked at it. I was thrilled to have a sample of his writing. And if memory served me right, it looked at lot like the writing on my late-night caller's note.

On the way home, I dropped off the note with Nate, at the police station.

"This is awesome!" He examined the note. "I'm not thrilled with you using yourself as bait. But good job. I'll have this compared to the other notes left by the killer."

"Thanks. I've got to go. Let me know."

He gave me a hug and a kiss before I went back out to my truck.

I spent the rest of the day catching up on my work for the FBI, but I was still jittery from the night before. I saw Bea's car pull into her driveway around 4:30. A few minutes later, she walked across the lawn and up the stairs to my front porch. I opened the door for her, and we settled on the sectional in the living room. Atlas was happy to see her, but after giving her a few sniffs, he settled down at my feet. We chatted about her trip for a few minutes, but I was just delaying the inevitable.

"What did you want to talk to me about?" Bea took a sip of the wine I'd poured.

"Atlas." I couldn't even look at her.

"What about him?"

I reached down and patted the top of his head.

"Would you consider letting me keep him?"

I'd decided to take Agent Phillips's advice and keep the dog.

Bea stared at me, and her jaw dropped. Then a huge smile crossed her face.

"Oh, honey! I'm so glad you brought that up."

"Huh?"

"I'd been thinking about how to ask you if you wanted him. He's way too much for me to handle, and I feel bad for him because I can't give him the exercise he needs. Of course you can keep him." She leaned over and gave me a hug.

I felt like I'd just won the lottery.

"Thanks, Bea. You can see him whenever you want."

She waved her hand. "Oh, I know that. I feel so free! Now I can take some of the trips I've wanted to take."

"Perfect." I smiled and looked down at Atlas. "Do you want to live with me?" I ruffled his ears.

He sat up and put his head on my lap, his tail thumping on the floor.

Bea and I chatted a few more minutes, before she left. She was tired from her trip and wanted to rest. We decided I'd pick up Atlas's bed, toys, and other items the next day.

When I got into bed that night, Atlas came up and laid down beside me, stretching his body against mine and letting out a big sigh. To me, it seemed that he knew he was home.

Karma, who'd meowed her displeasure at having the dog take up most the bed, curled up on my pillow above my head and kneaded her claws into my scalp as punishment. I didn't even care. I was content

The next morning, I took Atlas along while I went on my run. While he couldn't do the entire five miles—it would take time to build up his stamina—we managed a strong two and a half, and I was happy with that.

As much as I hated to admit it, the note the killer had left on my porch had rattled me more than I let on. I had my head on the swivel, looking out for the black car, the entire time Atlas and I had been on our run. I was frustrated. I didn't want to live this way, and it was time I did something about it.

As Atlas and I walked home, Bea stuck her head out her door and told me to come over for breakfast. She gave Atlas a bowl of water, and poured me a cup of coffee as I settled into a chair at the table.

"Have you made any progress on my genealogy?" She dished up our omelets.

"Not much." I hung my head. "Sorry, Bea. I'm up to my eyebrows in a murder."

She put her hand on my shoulder and sat my plate in front of me.

"It's okay, sweetie. You'll get to it, I'm sure."

Now I felt guiltier than ever. I sighed and dug into my omelet.

A little while later, I gathered Atlas's things up and took them to my house. I put his bed in my office, and his bowls in a corner of the kitchen where they were out of the way. I scrounged around in the basement and found a large wicker basket for his toys. I hoped he wouldn't eat the basket. But until I got something more suitable, it would have to do.

Since Bea had been so generous in giving me Atlas, the least I could do was to dig deeper into her family history and try to find someone who was a member of nobility. Besides, if I could find something, it might soften the blow of one of her ancestors being a prostitute. Maybe there was some kind of document which showed that Chief Inspector Martinelli just hauled in innocent girls and accused them of prostitution so he could use his position of power to blackmail them into sex. I mean, it wasn't unheard of, even by today's standards.

I tried several searches and came up empty. I then decided to enter the search term *Martinelli Inspector of Prostitutes*. After all, Professor Frost was an expert, and if Martinelli was that infamous, there had to be newspaper articles about him.

As hard as I tried, I couldn't find anything that referred to him as the Inspector of Prostitutes. In fact, there wasn't a hint of misconduct anywhere, and he was hailed as the man who was most likely to rid London of Jack the Ripper.

Martinelli was quoted in the papers as saying that he knew who Jack the Ripper was, but was waiting until he had irrefutable proof.

When I looked up at the clock, I realized most of the morning was gone, and I hadn't done a bit of work on the FBI file I'd been working on. *Damn it!*

I put Bea's stuff aside, vowing to work on it over the weekend, and turned my attention to another Jane Doe file. After about an hour, I stretched in my desk chair and got up to get something to eat. I noticed Karma was sitting on the floor in front of the murder board. She seemed to be fixated on something, but I couldn't pinpoint it. I laid on the floor next to her and followed her gaze. She was staring at the picture of Adrianna and the mystery man she'd been with at the grocery store.

An idea hit me, and I jumped up off the floor to get my cell phone.

"You're a genius!" I gave Karma a scratch behind the ears.

I texted the photograph to Agent Phillips and asked him if he could use the FBI's facial recognition program to identify him, and that it had to do with the murders in Hope Harbor. He texted back that he would. *Awesome!*

A couple hours later, I decided I needed a break, so I took Atlas out for a walk and to let him play at the park. He needed to burn off some energy, and the fresh air would do me good. I tucked Karma in the cat carrier I could put over my shoulder like a purse, and took her with us.

By the time I got back, Agent Phillips had texted with the name of the man Adrianna had been with—Stephen Bromley.

Hmm. That name hadn't come up in the investigation before. One of her ex-boyfriends, maybe? Or a current one?

I signed into the dating site and deleted the messages in my inbox from guys who wanted to hook up.

I'm not a hook-up kind of girl. Perverts.

I ran a search to see if Stephen was in the database, and within a few seconds, his profile popped up.

Damn it, Adrianna! Why are you still dating strange men when your life is being threatened? I shook my head.

Stephen's profile was generic—he liked animals, long walks on the beach, blah-blah-blah. I clicked out of the dating site and began to run him through the databases I used so I would have some real information.

He was a stockbroker—that was a step up from some of the other men she'd gone out with. He worked in Troy, a city that was centrally located between Hope Harbor and the cities the two murder victims had lived in. His financials looked good, and he didn't have a criminal record. He was definitely dateable, and I didn't see anything I would consider a red flag. The only thing that caught my attention is that he drove a black sedan. But so did a lot of other people.

I closed out the programs and went back to work on the FBI files. Checking out Adrianna's mystery man had been an exercise in futility, and I wanted to get something productive done before the end of the day.

I was getting closer to finding out who the Jane Doe was, when Karma leapt off the desk and trotted out of my office and down the hallway. Atlas, who'd been sleeping on his bed, perked up and followed Karma. Not wanting to be left behind, I followed him, and heard someone knock. I made Atlas sit, and opened the front door to find Chad Eastwick standing on my porch, holding a bouquet of flowers.

What the hell?

"Hi, Zoey." He held out the flowers. "These are for you. Can I talk to you, please?"

I took the flowers. "Sure. Come in."

I found it odd that Chad would show up soon after I'd found the mysterious note under my door mat. *What the hell does he want?*

He walked past me and stood by the kitchen island. He was fidgeting, and looked extremely uncomfortable.

"Sit, please." I waved toward one of the stools. "What's up?"

It took me a couple minutes to find a vase, and I filled it up with water for the flowers. I kept the island between us, and I was thrilled Atlas was there.

"I just wanted to apologize again for how I acted," he said. "It's been bugging me a lot. I was way out of line. I don't know what got into me. It was just that when you mentioned Adrianna, I saw red."

"It's okay, really." I smiled at him. "I get it. She's frustrating."

That wasn't a lie. Adrianna was one of the most exasperating women I'd ever met.

He nodded. "Can we start fresh?" He put his hand out. "Hi, I'm Chad Eastwick."

I giggled and shook his hand. "Hi, I'm Zoey Callaway."

"Well, Zoey Callaway, can I buy you dinner?"

I knew I should say no. He was a murder suspect.

Oh, what the heck. I might learn something.

"That would be wonderful, Mister Eastwick. Give me a few minutes to change."

We shared a laugh, and I retreated to my bedroom to get ready. A few minutes later, I was presentable for a date, and after I set the alarm, we disappeared into the night.

We ended up going to the Blue Bass. He'd never been there before, and I knew the food was amazing. Plus, it was on my turf, not his.

I found myself having a great time, just like before. Only, that time, I'd intentionally pushed his buttons by bringing up Adrianna. This time, I stayed far away from that subject. Unfortunately, this time, the subject found us.

We'd just finished our dinner and were having an after-dinner drink, when Adrianna came into the restaurant. She pushed past people to get to our table, which was in a corner by the front window, and put her hands on her hips, glaring at us.

Chad stood. "What are you doing here?" he whispered, and I wasn't sure if that was a good thing or a bad thing.

His jaw muscles clenched. She ignored him and turned her attention to me.

"I thought you were my friend! Why are you dating Chad?"

"We're not dating. We're having dinner. There's a difference."

"He's mine. Leave him alone!" she screamed.

"Adrianna, be quiet," Chad said. "You're making a scene, and we broke up a long time ago."

He grabbed her arm and tried to get her to move toward the door, but she wasn't having any of it. All the other diners were staring at us, and I could tell Chad was doing his best to diffuse the situation.

"It doesn't matter!" Adrianna shook off his grip. "You're still mine. Not hers. Mine! We weren't finished. You just gave up."

Before Chad could say anything, the manager came over to our table.

"Miss, you're going to have to leave."

Adrianna turned to face him. Her eyes were wide open, and her face was red.

She clenched her fists. "No. *She* has to leave." She pointed at me.

The manager looked toward the door and waved his hand. As soon as he did, a tall, stocky police officer entered the restaurant and strode over to Adrianna.

"Let's go, miss," he said.

"I'm not going anywhere without him." She looked at Chad.

"How much have you had to drink tonight, miss." The officer grabbed Adrianna's arm.

She tried to pull away from him, but his grip was strong.

"I'll make sure she gets home okay," he said to Chad.

Then he half-dragged, half-walked her out of the restaurant.

Chad looked at me and sat back down.

"I'm so sorry." He hung his head.

I smiled at him and reached across the table to squeeze his hand.

"Not your fault."

Chad paid the bill, and we rushed out of the restaurant.

"I'm really impressed," I said, as we walked through town, toward my house. "You didn't lose your temper with her."

"Thanks. I'm proud of you for not baiting her, like you did with me."

I chuckled. "Yeah, sorry about that."

We chatted the rest of the way back to my house, then said goodnight. When I got inside, I let Atlas out the back door— partly because he had to go potty, but mostly because I wanted him to do his usual patrol around the backyard.

No note writers, murderers, or Adrianna.

22

In the morning, I sipped coffee and browsed through emails before beginning working on the FBI files. My cell phone rang and I jumped. It was Adrianna.

"What's up?" I said.

I was still angry with her over last night's fiasco in the restaurant, but it was too early for a confrontation.

"Listen. About last night. Can we meet up and talk?"

I rolled my eyes. "Sure. Where?"

"How about the boardwalk by the beach? It's early, so there shouldn't be anyone around."

"Okay. I'll meet you there in a few minutes." I hung up without waiting for a reply.

As I got ready to leave, I wondered if she was going to apologize, or pick another spot. *And why meet on the boardwalk? It's secluded.*

When I got to the park, I headed down towards the boardwalk. In the distance, I saw Adrianna walking fast towards me.

When she saw me, she broke into a run and stopped just short of hitting me. Her face was red.

"Someone's following me!" she managed to gasp, between breaths.

She obviously didn't exercise, because that brief run had her sucking air.

"Stay here!" I headed in the direction she'd come from, and saw a man moving toward me.

I trotted towards him and was about to give him a piece of my mind when I realized it was Professor Frost.

"Hi, Professor. What are you doing out so early?"

I was relieved that it was only him. He's not exactly stalker material.

"Zoey!" He looked as surprised to see me as I was him. "What a pleasant surprise. I often take an early morning walk on the weekends, but rarely see anyone."

"My friend thought you were following her. She's the one I told you about. You know, Adrianna."

"Oh, the poor thing. Tell her I'm not at all scary."

We fell into step beside each other, and found Adrianna sitting on a bench.

"Adrianna, this is Professor Frost. He wasn't following you. He was just out for a walk."

He took Adrianna's hand. "I apologize for scaring you. I can assure you, I'm perfectly harmless."

"That's okay." Adrianna shook his hand, and blushed.

"Allow me to buy you two a cup of coffee. It's the least I can do after giving you such a fright."

We agreed, and chatted with him as we walked to Gil's. After settling in a booth and ordering coffee, we sat and exchanged small talk for a few minutes.

"So Zoey, how is dear Bea?" said the professor. "Have you found anything else out about her relative who was arrested for being a lady of the evening?"

"Bea is doing great. Thank you for asking. And no, I haven't. But here's a coincidence that should make it to the Guinness Book of Records." I clasped Adrianna's shoulder. "Adrianna has the last name Martinelli, the same as the chief inspector that arrested Bea's relative.

"Really?" Professor Frost looked Adrianna up and down, his eyebrows raised. "Martinelli, eh? Could be an Italian name. Maybe Portuguese. One in London. One right here in Hope Harbor—there's a migration for you."

Adrianna giggled. "Nice to have a famous namesake."

"Sadly, Martinelli was a crooked cop," the professor said. "Sorry to pop your bubble."

"He was?"

"Yes. He arrested innocent people, and slandered others. Disgusting." His voice was filled with distain. "Yet his superiors thought he was a god." He shook his head.

"That's a shame," Adrianna said. "I so hate injustice!"

I looked at her and tried to swallow a laugh, given the events of last night, but I only succeeded in my coffee going down the wrong way, causing me to have a coughing fit.

"Oh, my dear! Are you okay?" The professor got up from his seat and stood beside me, patting my back.

I waved him off. "I'm fine. Thank you."

After chatting a few more minutes, the professor said he had to go grade papers, and left Adrianna and I alone in the booth.

"So what in the hell was that about last night?" I picked up a menu to see what I wanted for breakfast.

"I'm sorry." She hung her head. "I'd had too much to drink, and when I saw you with Chad, I just lost it."

"Being drunk isn't an excuse You embarrassed everyone. But most of all, yourself. I mean, having to be escorted out by the police? Really, Adrianna?"

"I know. I felt horrible. I really am sorry."

"Chad and I were just out to dinner. It wasn't a date. Men and women are allowed to be friends and have a meal together, you know." I glared at her.

"True." She sat back in the booth, deflated. "Chad is just a sore spot for me. It was such a bad break up."

I couldn't argue with that. But after her performance last night, I wasn't sure any more about who broke up with who, and why. I held my response until after the waitress served us our food and left.

"If it was a bad break up, then why do you care who he's with?" I dug into my omelet.

"I don't. I just didn't want you to get hurt the way I did." She smiled at me.

I wasn't buying it for a second. Evidently, I hadn't heard the real story from either of them on what exactly happened between them, but I was sure it wasn't pretty.

"I'm a big girl, Adrianna. I can take care of myself. I have to go."

I couldn't take any more of her lies and excuses. I grabbed my bill and paid at the register. Without looking back, I left and walked home.

It was the weekend, and as much as I needed to get some work done, I just couldn't concentrate. I sat and stared at the murder board for I don't know how long. No matter how hard I tried, nothing made sense. I was obviously missing something. I wished Uncle Felix was still alive. He would have been able to figure it out.

I sighed and shut down my computer. Perhaps an outing would help clear my mind. I looked at the calendar on the Hope Harbor website and found out the church was having a garage sale in the auditorium of the Catholic school.

Cool!

I decided to drive into town instead of walking, because you never know what you're going to find at a garage sale, and if I got carried away, I'd need my truck to take home all my treasures.

When I got to the church, it took me a few minutes to find a place to park, but I finally found a spot in the parking lot of an old building that used to be a funeral home. As I headed to the entrance, Pam Davis fell into step next to me, and we exchanged greetings.

"How are things at the historical society?" I slowed my pace to match hers.

"Not bad. We need to set up a time to get together and plan the additional witch cemetery research. It's almost warm enough for you to go back out there."

"I know. I can't wait!"

The witch cemetery had become a pet project of mine since I had worked on it the year before. There was still so much to be learned about the women who were buried there.

"Let's set something up next week," I said.

Pam nodded.

When we got to the entrance, Pam headed for the houseware section, and I made a beeline for the books.

"Hey, Zoey." Frank Dixon tapped me on the shoulder.

I wasn't surprised that he'd beat me to the book section.

"Hey, Frank. How's the cat and the store?"

"Both are good." He chuckled. "I'm telling you, that cat was the best decision I've made in a long time. The customers love him, and I can't imagine life without him."

"I told you." I laughed. "So how are things between you and Bea? Are you still seeing each other?"

"Yes, we are." He blushed. "In fact…" he paused and looked around to see if anyone was in earshot, "I'm thinking of asking her to marry me."

I gasped and almost dropped two autographed first editions I'd picked up from one of the tables.

"Are you serious?"

"Yes." His face clouded over. "You don't approve?"

"Of course I do! I'm so happy for you." I gave him a hug.

"*Whew!* Will you come with me to pick out a ring? You'd know what a woman would like better than I would."

I felt honored that he would ask me.

"Name the time," I said.

"How about after we leave the sale?"

"Perfect."

We parted and continued to look around. I found a few books, a kitchen strainer, and some knick-knacks that I could put in the spare bedroom. It needed sprucing up.

Frank met me in the parking lot, and after we put his items in his car, he got into my Jeep and we headed to a jewelry store a few towns away. In Hope Harbor, everybody knew everybody, and if you forgot what you were doing, you'd only have to ask someone and they could tell you. Frank was afraid if we shopped local, word would get back to Bea, and he wanted it to be a surprise.

Three stores later, we both decided on a vintage ring. I knew Bea preferred white gold or platinum, and this ring was perfect. The simple setting held a large emerald cut diamond surrounded by small rubies. It was stunning, and I knew Bea would love it.

The clerk gave us a few sideways glances as I tried the rings on, and neither of us bothered to correct the salesperson's assumptions, but we did exchange a few knowing smiles.

"Now, not a word, young lady," Frank said, when I dropped him back off at his car.

"I know. But do it soon. I'm terrible at secrets." I laughed.

I cleaned up the knick-knacks I'd purchased, and arranged them in the guest room. Then I spent some time putting protective covers over the dustjackets of the books, and cataloging them, before placing them on one of my bookshelves.

I wondered if Bea was going to say yes to Frank, and how she would react to having a cat instead of a dog. Frank and Bea both deserved happiness, and they were perfect for each other. Now, if I could just find my special someone.

I thought I'd found him in Jason, but that didn't go as planned. As nice as Nate was, other than murder, I didn't see that we had a lot in common.

I sighed at the dimness of my prospects in the love department, and pulled out the FBI file I'd been working on. Dealing with murder victims and criminals all day wasn't doing much for my mood. While I loved the work, I tended to get emotionally involved with the victims I was trying to identify, and it was depressing. I needed some fun.

I texted Shannon to see if she was busy and wanted to do something. She said her husband was working tonight, and she was bored to death. She suggested we grab some dinner and go to a movie. I agreed.

A few minutes later, she showed up at my house and we looked online at movie showtimes. We decided on a psychological thriller and picked a time that allowed us have dinner first. We piled into my truck and headed to a Mexican restaurant that was close to the theatre. Neither of us had eaten there before, and were dying to try the food. As I drove, I noticed there was a car behind me that was shadowing my every turn and lane change.

"Damn it!" I banged my hands on the steering wheel.

"What?" Shannon said.

I glanced in the rearview mirror again. "We're being followed."

Shannon twisted in her seat and looked out the back window. She squinted, trying to make out any details.

"It's too dark. I can't see who's driving."

After checking my mirrors to make sure I was clear, I swerved across two lanes and into a turn-around to head the opposite way. The vehicle behind me did the same thing and ended up right on my bumper at the light. I had a slight opening in traffic, and made a sharp turn into the lane closest to me. The vehicle behind me, couldn't follow because of traffic.

I pulled into the driveway of a shopping center and drove to the back of the buildings. I backed in alongside a large dumpster and cut the engine so we were sitting in complete darkness and silence.

A few minutes passed with no activity, so I turned on my vehicle and drove out of the shopping center, towards the restaurant, keeping a close eye on who was behind me.

"Going out with you is never boring. I'll give you that." Shannon chuckled.

"Yeah." I pulled into a parking spot at the restaurant. "Welcome to my world."

We got seated and ordered a pitcher of margaritas to sip on while we looked at the menu.

"Who do you think that was?" Shannon said.

"Hard to say." I shrugged.

The waitress dropped off our drinks and took our order.

"Are that many people out to get you?" Shannon's eyes got wide.

I thought about the work I was doing for the FBI, and Agent Phillips's veiled warnings. Plus, I was up to my eyeballs in a murder case.

"Of course not," I said. "It was probably just some creep."

Dinner was great, and the movie wasn't bad. By the time we got back to my house, it was after midnight. We said goodbye, and as I entered my house, I noticed the front door was ajar.

I forgot to set the alarm! Where's Atlas, and why isn't he going crazy?

I stood frozen in place for a few seconds, and prayed Atlas would come bounding to the front door. But he didn't. It was deathly quiet.

And where's Karma? Why isn't the porch light on?

The glow from my cell phone revealed shards of glass from the broken bulb laying at my feet. My heart was pounding out of my chest, and a cold wave of panic started at my toes and worked up my body. Within a few seconds, I was trembling.

I was having an argument in my head as to whether or not I should go into the house, or call for help. I reached into the house and flicked on the light switch for the living room. It was empty. I took a tentative step into the house and stood stock-still, listening for any noise.

Nothing.

Every fiber of my being wanted to streak across the street to bang on Jason's door for help, but I'd done that enough lately.

Come on, Z. You're not a helpless female. You can do this!

I tiptoed across the living room and grabbed the fireplace poker. I heard a noise from my office, and stopped in my tracks. If that's where my intruder was, I needed more than a piece of metal in my hand, so I crept to my bedroom and grabbed the gun out of my nightstand.

My office door was closed, but I knew I had left it open. When I reached it, I took a deep breath and released the safety on my gun. I slowly turned the doorknob, then pushed the door open and turned on the light. I saw Atlas laid out on the floor. He wasn't moving. Karma was standing on my desk, hissing, her hair standing on end.

"Atlas!" I rushed over to him and crouched down beside him.

He was breathing. I tried to wake him up, but no response. I had to get him to an emergency vet, and I couldn't do it by myself.

I reached into my coat pocket for my cell phone, but it wasn't there.

Damn it! Must have set it down when I was getting the gun.

I picked up the gun and ran down the hallway to my bedroom. With trembling fingers, I dialed Nate's number.

He answered on the second ring. "Zoey?"

"Help!" was all I managed to squeak out.

The line went dead, and a few short minutes later, I heard sirens. A police car pulled up in front of my house, followed by Nate's truck. I let them in, and led Nate down the hallway to my office.

"Help me get him into the car," I said.

He picked Atlas up and carried him out to his truck. He opened the back door and laid him on the backseat.

"Stay with him." Nate disappeared back into the house.

He joined me a minute or two later and used the lights and sirens on his truck to get us to the vet in record time.

I explained what happened, to Dr. Maddox. He examined Atlas and took a blood sample. It seemed to take forever to find out what was wrong.

"It looks like he got into your sleeping pills, Zoey," said Dr. Maddox. "You really should be more careful."

"But I don't take any, and there's none in the house." I stroked Atlas's head.

"I'm going to pump his stomach and give him an IV. He should be fine by morning. You can pick him up then."

I breathed a sigh of relief. Maybe adopting Atlas hadn't been such a great idea, given that in less than forty-eight hours I'd almost gotten him killed.

I kissed Atlas goodbye and gave him a hug.

"Hang in there, boy," I whispered in his ear.

Nate and I walked to his truck in silence.

"You ready to talk about tonight?" He backed out of the parking space.

On the way back to the house, I told him about the car that had followed me earlier that night, and my actions when I got back to the house.

"Whose buttons did you push this time?" He gave me a sideways glance.

"I honestly don't know." I shrugged.

I told him about how Adrianna reacted when she saw me with Chad, and my meeting with Daniel.

Something was missing. Why would the killer break into my house just to drug Atlas? Maybe he drugged Atlas so he could get into the house without incident. But why? Maybe it was to show me he could get to me anytime he wanted, and there was nothing I could do about it. The thought sent shockwaves up and down my spine.

When we got back to my house, the police car was still there, and a crime scene vehicle was parked in my driveway.

I got out of the truck, and Shannon and Bea rushed to me from the front porch.

"Are you okay?" Shannon said.

"How's Atlas?" Bea said.

"Atlas is going to be fine," I told Bea. "I'm pissed," I said to Shannon.

They nodded and walked with me into the house.

Jason was sitting at the kitchen island, talking to Agent Phillips. *What the hell is Agent Phillips doing here?*

The crime scene technicians looked like they'd about finished up. Jason gave me a nasty look and shook his head. Agent Phillips latched onto my upper arm and led me into my office. He shut the door behind us and led me over to my chair. I sat, and he put the spare chair in front of me. He looked at me for a long time after he sat.

"This is my fault," he said. "I should have acted sooner."

"What are you talking about?"

"I got a call a couple days ago. Whoever called tried to change their voice. It sounded muffled. Our experts think it may be a Canadian, as he spoke with a pretend Bronx accent straight out of the movies. Anyway, he said, 'You didn't call Zoey Callaway off. I'm sure the FBI is really going to miss her.'"

His words gave me chills.

"Is this about the whole Adrianna mess, or the files I'm working on for you?"

He ran his hand through his hair. "I'm not sure. But if I had to guess, it's about Adrianna. At any rate, I want to put you in a safe house immediately."

"No!" I jumped out of the chair, fists clenched at my side, and started pacing around the room. "I'm fine. If this guy wanted to kill me, he would have done it already."

Agent Phillips shook his head. "Not necessarily. Did it ever occur to you that he's playing a game of cat and mouse with you?"

"And what pleasure or value would he get from that?"

"It's a power trip. These types of men like to scare women. But they end up hurting them later."

I turned to look at him. He had a good point. That's exactly what it felt like.

I went back over to my chair and sat. "So I need to outsmart him."

"No, you need to let me protect you until we catch this guy. It's too dangerous."

"What other choice do you have?" I stared into his eyes. "Clearly this guy wants to play, and if I can keep him busy, then maybe, just maybe, another innocent person doesn't have to be slaughtered."

His shoulders slumped. "Honestly, I do think you're our best chance at luring this guy out into the open. He seems fascinated by you."

I nodded. "So what do I do?"

"We need to figure out a way to get a message to him. It may make him panic if he thinks you know who he is. That could cause him to make a mistake." Agent Phillips stroked his chin. "I'm just not sure you're up to the task. It's too dangerous."

"Dangerous?" I yelled, and leapt out of my chair. "Obviously I'm already in danger. The longer this guy is out there, the more dangerous it becomes. Let me do this."

He sighed, and I knew I'd won.

"Don't misunderstand. I'm not going to let you do this alone and without protection. There are conditions."

"Such as?"

He leaned forward in his chair. "Such as, an agent will be tailing you at all times, and we will be monitoring your house. You are not to even attempt to shake your surveillance, understand?" He gave me a stern look.

He knew me so well.

"I understand. What else? You're not going to fire me, are you?"

He chuckled. "No, I'm not going to fire you. I admire your determination."

That was a relief. I loved my job.

"Wait, it's not going to be Jason, is it? Because if it is, you can forget it."

"No, it's not Jason. You take a day or two and think it over. In the meantime, I'm going to have someone keep an eye on you. Deal?" He held out his hand.

I shook it. "Deal."

We left my office, and everyone looked at us expectantly. Neither of us said anything. Agent Phillips excused himself and left. Shannon and Bea both went home as well. I told Jason to go home, and led him toward the door.

"Call me for anything," he said.

"I will. Thanks."

Once the crime scene techs and the policeman left, I locked the door and set the alarm. It was after 1:00 a.m., and I was exhausted.

Sleep was hard to come by, and the picture of Atlas laid out on the floor encroached on my thoughts. As upsetting as the entire evening had been, I wasn't scared. I was furious.

I finally drifted off to sleep, thinking about my conversation with Agent Phillips. *How the hell am I going to send the killer a message when I don't even know who the killer is? My big mouth really got me into a mess this time. So how the hell do I do this?*

As I got ready for my run the next morning, I was hoping that whoever was assigned to keep an eye on me was up to the task. I did my stretching exercises on the front porch, popped in my earbuds, and set out at a trot. By the time I turned the corner, heading toward town, I noticed a car creeping down the road behind me. *Must be my tail.*

I turned around and ran to the car, which had come to a stop, and tapped on the passenger side window. When the window went down, I saw a young, handsome man behind the wheel. He was wearing jeans and a white polo shirt with the FBI logo on it. He looked at me with intense blue eyes.

"Hi, Miss Callaway. I'm Travis."

I was jogging in place next to the car. "Well, Travis. You're going to have a hard time following me in that car once we get into traffic. What's wrong? You not up to the task?" I smiled at him and took off down the street.

Within seconds, Travis was running alongside me. I did my normal five miles, and he did a decent job of keeping up. When we got back to my house, I got us each a bottle of water, and we sat in the chairs on the front porch.

"You okay?" I looked at him.

His face was red, and he was gasping for air.

"Fine." He waved his hand. "Do you think tomorrow we could stop at three miles, until I get used to this?"

I laughed. "We'll see."

My cell phone rang.

"Hello?"

"Zoey, it's Doctor Maddox. Atlas is doing great, and he's ready to go home. You can pick him up anytime."

After my shower, I jumped into my Jeep and raced to the vet's office, with Travis following me. As I checked to make sure he was keeping up, I realized that being under surveillance all the time was going to be a pain, and seriously cramp my style.

Atlas gave me an enthusiastic greeting, and I was thrilled to see him back to his big goofy self. When we got home, I gave him some extra treats and he settled down on his bed in my office. Even Karma seemed happy to see him, because she rubbed up against his chest and purred.

I made some coffee and headed to my office. I had to come up with a plan to draw the killer out. I was good at cat and mouse games when it came to doing skip tracing work on my computer. But I wasn't sure how that would translate to this situation.

I turned around and looked at my murder board. I had a lot of suspects, and it was time to start eliminating some.

Chad was a great suspect, except I hadn't found a link between him and the other two women that'd been murdered. But maybe that was the point. Maybe there wasn't a connection between the killer and the first two victims. After all, his real target was Adrianna.

After letting that theory roam around in my head for a bit, it made sense that the other women were just targets of choice. If so, that would let Daniel off the hook. While he did go out with all of them, he didn't seem the type that would commit cold-blooded murder.

So that would leave Chad, who would be the best suspect—especially if the other two women were just random targets. But he didn't own a black car. He had a pickup. Just to be sure, I ran Chad through one of my databases and found a black sedan registered to him.

I sat back in my chair, astounded. That information just moved Chad to the top of my suspect list. Now it was time to test that theory. The question was, *How?*

It's been my experience that if you work on something else, your brain will come up with a solution to the real problem—how to bait Chad.

I spent the rest of my day working on files for the FBI, and stopped only for lunch and to let out the dog. Poor Travis must be bored to tears sitting in the car, watching nothing. I was sure this wasn't what he envisioned when he'd signed up with the FBI.

By the time late afternoon rolled around, I had hatched half a plan on how to deal with Chad. The rest I'd have to play by ear. Probably not the best solution, but it was the best I had.

I called Chad and asked him if he wanted to meet for dinner, which he agreed to. He suggested a restaurant in Algonac, and I agreed. As I got ready for my date, I had to admit that I felt a braver knowing Travis would be watching me.

Before I got in my Jeep, I told Travis where we were going in case we got separated in traffic. When I got to the restaurant, Chad was waiting for me in his truck. As soon as I parked, he got out of his vehicle and opened my truck door for me. *Such a gentleman.*

I'd decided to start out slow and work my way up to the conversation I wanted to have with him. However, he had other ideas, and brought up Adrianna as soon as we'd been served our drinks.

"The police came and talked to me again about Adrianna and you." His voice was calm, which made me uneasy.

"Me?"

"Yes. Do you really think I'm capable of breaking into your house and drugging your dog? I didn't even know you had a dog."

I saw a vein pop out on his neck, which told me he was struggling to control his temper. I glanced around the restaurant and saw Travis sitting three tables away from us.

"I didn't say anything to the police about you last night. But let's face it, you are probably on top of their suspect list because of your connection to Adrianna."

"It always comes back to my connection with Adrianna." He ran his hand through his hair. "No matter how hard I try, I'm not going to be rid of that bitch until one of us is dead."

I sat back in my chair and stared at him.

That was probably the dumbest thing a murder suspect could say, and I wasn't sure Chad was that dumb.

24

let the comment slide. My head was telling me he could be the murderer. But in my heart, I just didn't buy it.

We finished our dinner and agreed to meet at a bar in downtown Algonac. I went in and looked around for Travis, but couldn't find him. *Maybe he's waiting in his car.*

It was 1:00 a.m. when Chad escorted me to my truck. It was one of the best Saturday nights I'd had in a long time. He gave me a sweet kiss goodnight, and I pulled out of the parking lot. I saw a pickup pull out behind me, but it wasn't Travis—he drove a car.

As I drove home, I realized that being under surveillance was a double-edged sword. On one hand, I did feel safer knowing help was close. But on the other hand, when you aren't sure the person following you is FBI, you feel vulnerable.

The pickup didn't follow me all the way home. It turned off on a side street just outside of Hope Harbor. For the last three miles, I didn't see a car of any kind, which made me nervous, and I sped up.

What the hell happened to my protection? Did the killer get to them?

I thought about turning around and making sure Travis was okay, but I just wanted to go home. I pulled into a gas station and texted Agent Phillips.

He said everything was fine, and just because I didn't see them didn't mean they weren't there.

Huh?

I finally got home and pulled into the garage. I went in through the backdoor and let Atlas out. When he came back in, I locked the door and set the alarm. Then I went through the house, checking all the doors and windows. As I did, I looked for anything that seemed out of place. The murderer had made me paranoid. This had to stop.

Atlas, Karma, and I crawled into bed and snuggled up together. It felt like a family, and given the dim prospects for my love life, it may be the only family I would ever have.

When I got up Sunday morning, the last thing I wanted to do was go for a run, so I started some coffee and took a shower. As I shampooed my hair, I thought about all that had happened in the past couple weeks, and I felt bad for walking out on Adrianna at the restaurant the last time we'd met. Maybe I'd pop by her house and make nice. After all, she was my only link to the killer, and I knew there was something she wasn't telling me.

By the time I'd gotten dressed, it had started to rain, so I decided to drive over to Adrianna's instead of walk. I pulled in behind her car and tried to dodge the raindrops as I sprinted to the front porch. I rang the doorbell a few times, but there was no response. When I banged on the front door, it swung open.

I froze. A shot of adrenaline pulsed through my body.

"Adrianna?" I yelled into the house, but was met with silence.

I looked down the street, but didn't see anything that seemed out of place. A car had parked against the curb, and a man was in it. Probably my surveillance.

Maybe she was in the shower and couldn't hear me.

I entered the house and looked around. The end tables in the living room had been knocked over, their contents scattered across the floor.

My pulse quickened, and my heart felt like it was going to beat out of my chest.

"Adrianna!"

I ran down the hallway toward her bedroom, and saw her laid out on the bed. The bedclothes were soaked in blood, and her eyes were wide open and empty. Her arms had been folded across her chest with a gold, heart-shaped candy box resting on them, with a gift tag that said, *For Zoey*.

I screamed and put my hands up to my face to block the sight. A man I didn't know ran into the room, gun in hand. Fear gripped my body, and I backed further into the room, searching for a way out.

"Zoey! I'm Corey, from the FBI. It's okay," he said, in a soft voice, and held out his hand toward me. "Come on. Let's get you out of here."

I couldn't move. I was frozen.

"Prove it," I squeaked.

He reached into his coat pocket and held up his FBI identification.

"Come on." He held out his hand again.

This time, I put my hand in his and he pulled me gently towards him. He wrapped his arm around my trembling body and led me out of the house, to a chair on the front porch.

"Stay here," he said.

He took his cell phone out of his coat pocket and made a call. Seconds later, I heard sirens. Corey crossed the porch in two strides and knelt down in front of me.

"Are you okay?"

I'd had a few minutes to recover from the shock, but I was still shaking. I couldn't speak, but I managed to nod. He took off his coat and put it around me.

Nate and two patrol cars came to a screeching halt in front of Adrianna's house, followed by an ambulance and a crime scene technician van. Corey introduced himself to Nate and came back to where I was seated. He put a protective hand on my shoulder.

Nate disappeared into the house, while the patrol officers set up a perimeter around the house with crime scene tape.

Nate emerged from the house and came over to me. Corey excused himself to call Agent Phillips, and Nate sat in the chair next to me.

"Tell me everything, from the second you got here."

I told him everything I did and saw, and he wrote everything down in a little black notebook.

"Was there a note?" I said.

"No. Just the candy box with your name on it."

I nodded. "Did you open the box yet?"

Nate hung his head and didn't look at me.

"Tell me." I squeezed his hand.

"Adrianna's heart was in the box," he whispered.

My stomach did flip-flops, and I fought off a wave of nausea. I had no words. Just nodded.

"She must have put up one hell of a fight," Nate said. "Are you going to be okay? I have to get back in there."

"I'm fine."

He got up and nodded to Corey, who came and sat next to me.

"I'm sorry." He touched my arm.

I barely heard him. I replayed the scene in my head over and over so I wouldn't forget anything.

"Can I go home now?" I looked at him.

"I'll find out." He got up and went to the front door to speak to the policeman monitoring who was going in and out of the house. "We can go. Nate said he'll come over later."

When I pulled into my driveway, I saw Agent Phillips and Jason waiting for me on the front porch. *Peachy.* I just wanted to be alone.

Ignoring them, I unlocked the front door and turned off the alarm before starting coffee and letting Atlas out into the backyard. Agent Phillips came into the kitchen and helped me pour the coffee. He handed me my cup, and I sat on one of the bar stools.

"It could have been you," Jason said, and the muscles in his neck flexed. "It's like you're a murder magnet. If there's a dead body in Hope Harbor, Lord knows you're going to either find it or be in the middle of it."

"Jason! That's enough." Agent Phillips glared at him. "Go home. You're not needed here. She's been through enough."

Jason opened his mouth to say something, but thought better of it. He took a step towards me, but Corey blocked his path. Jason shook his head and stormed out the door. Slammed it behind him. The noise made me to jump.

Agent Phillips took my arm and led me back to my office.

"Type everything out before you forget it."

I nodded and turned on my computer. Karma came into the office, jumped up on my lap, lay down and started to purr. As if she could sense I needed her close.

For the next half-hour, I was completely focused on getting the images out of my head to translate into words. I tried to keep my emotion out of it and stick to the facts, but it wasn't as easy as I thought it would be.

I felt horrible that my last words to Adrianna were out of anger, but there was nothing I could do about that now. The only thing I could do was help find out who did this to her.

I printed my statement and handed it to Agent Phillips, who scanned through it.

"Good. Who was the guy you were out with last night?"

How does he know? Oh, right, the surveillance team.

"Chad Eastwick." I nodded toward the murder board.

Agent Phillips got up to take a closer look at his picture and information, then turned around to face me.

"Your main suspect?"

"Yes." I dislodged Karma from my lap and went over to join Agent Phillips. "It's possible he drove into Hope Harbor after we left the bar, and killed Adrianna."

"True." He stroked his chin. "But?"

"But I don't think he did." I went back to my chair and sat. "Adrianna and Chad had a bad breakup, and I can't figure out who was stalking who. But that doesn't make him a killer."

Why am I defending him again? Damn it!

"Okay. So once we talk to Nate and get more information about Adrianna's murder," Agent Phillips said, "it's time to start over. He will have to look for other suspects."

I nodded.

"I'm gonna to go. Corey will be here, and I'm going to send another agent over as well." He took my hand to help me out of my chair. "You should get some rest."

I couldn't argue. I was emotionally spent. All I wanted to do was crawl into bed and pull the covers over my head.

I locked the door behind him and set the alarm before going back to bed. I needed time to process everything that'd happened.

I woke up to someone pounding on my front door.

It was Nate. I glanced at the clock in the kitchen and saw it was after 4:30. I'd slept most the day away.

"I've been trying to call you," he said.

"Sorry." I shrugged. "So what's up? Do you have any new leads? What's the time of death?"

Nate held his hands up. "Whoa. Slow down. Do you have any coffee?"

"I'll make some." I went into the kitchen.

Nate sat on one of the bar stools and took his notebook out of his jacket pocket.

"The coroner estimates that she was killed between 10:00 p.m. and midnight last night."

"Well, that eliminates Chad Eastwick. I was with him in Algonac. We were together until almost 1:00 a.m."

Nate made a note. I poured us coffee and sat next to him.

"We found fingerprints on the candy box." He sat down his notebook and turned to face me.

He flexed his hands, and a pained look crossed his face.

"They were Jason's."

"Jason!" I felt like I'd been sucker punched in the stomach.

I was lightheaded, and found it hard to breathe. My mind flashed back to seeing Jason at Adrianna's house a few nights ago.

"I'm having him picked up and taken to the station." Nate hung his head. "I have to get back."

"I-it can't be him. Where's his motive?"

Nate shrugged. "That's what I'm about to find out." He got off the stool and went to the front door. "Stay home today. Lock the door and set your alarm. I'll call you later."

I nodded and did as he instructed, but my sense of safety had been shattered.

It was 6:30 when I saw Jason coming down the sidewalk toward his house. He must have walked home from the police station—it was only a few blocks away. He glanced toward my house before disappearing through his front door.

I hung my head and fought back tears. My heart broke for him, but I still wondered how the candy box with his fingerprints on it ended up in Adrianna's hands after she was murdered.

After dinner, I worked on another one of the FBI files, but my heart wasn't in it. I shut down my computer around nine and went to bed.

It had dawned on me sometime in the early morning hours that Adrianna may not have any living relatives, and I didn't want her to be buried in a pauper's grave. So I called Nate, and he said they hadn't been able to locate any relatives. As soon as I knew the funeral home was open, I called and scheduled to meet with them.

The morning was cold, wet, and dark. Ominous storm clouds rolled across the sky as I climbed into my Jeep and headed into town. Christie's Funeral Home was a block off the main drag and housed in an old building that used to be a bar, ages before. The building stood two stories tall and was constructed out of bricks that had been made right here in Hope Harbor, back in the 1800s.

I found a place to park in front, and opened the heavy wooden door to enter. Victorian furniture decorated the large reception area, and reproduction wallpaper from the 1800s adorned the walls. I felt like I'd just stepped a hundred years back in time.

David Christie, a fifth-generation funeral director, came out of his office. His pale skin and blond hair was in glaring contrast to the black suit and black tie he wore on his tall, slim body. His polished black shoes didn't make a sound as he strode across the carpet.

"Zoey." He took my hand in both of his.

His hands were soft, like baby skin.

"I'm so sorry to hear about the loss of your friend."

"Thank you." I gently extracted my hand.

"Let's go into my office and talk." He stepped back and allowed me to go first.

He took my elbow to gently guide me in the right direction. When we reached his office, he pulled out the chair across from his massive tiger oak desk, and waited for me to sit before going behind his desk and settling in a large chair.

David went over all the prices and other important items before escorting me to a separate room where all the coffins were displayed. I didn't know whether Adrianna wanted to be buried or cremated. But since cremation was the least expensive option, I settled for that. Not that I was cheap. I had limited funds.

I chose a pink cremation coffin for her, and a blue one for her father, who'd been left in the Northwoods to rot away into nothing but bones, and didn't receive a proper service. So I opted to have him cremated as well. It was the least I could do.

I chose two beautiful urns—if urns can be beautiful—to house their remains. Adrianna's was the more modern, with a pattern that reminded me of the wind. It seemed to suit her. For her father, I chose a dignified mahogany urn that was polished to a glimmering sheen. I had no earthly idea what I was going to do with them, but it seemed too sad to just throw their ashes into the sky, or have them disposed of in some anonymous fashion.

My next stop was to see Father Michael at St. Agatha's. I had set the funerals for Saturday, at the funeral home. I explained the situation to the priest—an awkward conversation—and he agreed to officiate.

The town was deserted, and the rain had finally stopped as I drove the two short blocks from the church to the flower store. I ordered an arrangement of flowers for Adrianna and her father to be delivered to the funeral home.

David Christie had said he would make the arrangements to pick up the bodies from the medical examiner's office and get me the death certificates.

I got back into my Jeep and fished for the key to Adrianna's house, but couldn't find it. *What the hell?*

I emptied out my purse and checked all the nooks and crannies, but the key was gone!

I called Nate and told him that I needed to get into Adrianna's house to pick out some proper clothes for her funeral, and that the key she'd given me had disappeared.

"Are you sure you just didn't misplace it?"

"Positive." I shook my head. "I'll check when I get home. Maybe it just fell out of my bag."

"I'll meet you there in a few minutes. Oh, by the way…Jason said he'd bought the candy for you. Something about a date night, and that he left them in his truck. When he got up the morning Adrianna's body was found, his truck window had been busted out, and the candy stolen."

"Sounds kind of lame." *Date night? We've never had one before.*

Nate chuckled. "It did to me to. But his truck window had been busted. Of course, he could have done it himself."

"Okay. I'll see you soon."

When I pulled into Adrianna's driveway, even the house looked sad. The grass hadn't been cut, and the curtains were closed. Mail was spilling out of her mailbox by the front door, so I grabbed it and leafed through while I waited for Nate. I tossed the bills in the front seat of my truck because the attorney who was handling her probate would need to submit them to the court. Once I knew who he was, I'd drop it off to them.

Nate showed up a few minutes later and gave me a hug when he joined me on the porch.

"That was really nice of you to arrange for their funerals. I'll be there and get the word out."

"Thanks." I smiled up at him.

He pulled the house keys out of his pocket and unlocked the door, then stepped aside to let me go first. I paused just inside the front door and looked around. Everything appeared to be in the same state it was on the morning I found her body.

When I got to the bedroom door, I stopped. Had I really thought I could just march in here and get her clothes without having a reaction?

Zoey, sometimes you are such an idiot.

I bowed my head and took a minute to push out of my mind the visions of Adrianna's corpse lying on the bed.

Nate touched my shoulder. "You okay? Want me to do this?"

"Oh, heavens no." I shook my head. "I want the clothes to at least match."

I forced myself to move into the room. Diverting my gaze from the bed, I stepped over to her dresser and started opening the drawers to get her some undergarments. I have to say, I was shocked at the ultra-sexy and skimpy bras and panties in the top drawer of her dresser. She didn't seem the type. I couldn't help but notice the designer labels, and wondered how she afforded such expensive lingerie on her low salary.

In the next drawer, I found what appeared to be everyday lingerie. I didn't want to give David Christie at the funeral home a heart attack, so I chose a plain pair of black undies and a plain black bra.

"Damn it!" I shut the drawer. "I forgot to bring something to put her clothes in."

Nate was leaning against the door jamb, watching me.

"I have a large paper evidence bag in my truck. Will that do?"

I glanced over at him. "Perfect. Thanks!"

He disappeared, and I heard the front door open and shut as I pulled her double closet doors open. Since I wasn't familiar with her closet or wardrobe, I figured the easiest way to find something would be to push all the clothes to one side and go through them one by one until I found something suitable.

I had to admit, I had clothes envy as I plowed through her designer apparel. There were many dresses that I didn't think were suitable for a funeral, but I pulled out a few things that could work. Even then, I kept going because I was hoping I'd come across something that wasn't too casual or too fancy. I wanted to find the perfect outfit.

The last item hanging in the closet was a black dress that looked like it would work. I lifted the hanger off the rod and held the dress up in front of me to see where the hemline would fall. Adrianna and I had been close to the same height, so if it wasn't too short for me, it would be fine for her.

The length hit me just below the knees, which told me it would hit just above the knees on Adrianna. *Perfect.*

As I went to hang the other clothes back up, I noticed the drywall on the sidewall of the closet had been cut in such a way that it formed a small door.

Nate reappeared in the doorway, carrying a paper evidence bag. "Here you go." He came over to where I was standing.

"Set it on the floor. Look at this?" I pointed toward the closet.

He followed my finger and furrowed his brow when he saw the door-like cuts in the drywall. I reached out and pulled back the flap of drywall. Laying on one of the cross beams was a little black book and a cloth makeup bag. I grabbed the book and pulled it out of the closet to look at it in better light. We exchanged quizzical looks.

Written in Adrianna's neat hand were what looked like initials, dates, locations, and dollar amounts. I handed the book to Nate and reached back in to get the makeup bag. Unzipped the top and found what had to be thousands of dollars.

"What the hell?" I looked at Nate.

He whistled. "I better get the crime scene boys over here again." He frowned. "They obviously missed some things."

He took the bag out of my hand and left the room. I followed. He went over to the kitchen counter and started counting the cash. I picked up the black book and examined it in closer detail. Couldn't make heads nor tails out of it, but I knew enough to know it didn't contain the type of information that a bookie would write down.

I reached into my purse on the counter, grabbed my cell phone and took a picture of the first page of the notebook.

"You know," he said, "you really shouldn't be doing that."

"I know." I didn't dare look at him. "Do you want me to stop?"

"Yes. Actually, I do. You don't have to erase the picture you took, but no more. It's evidence in a murder investigation, and I could get fired."

He snatched away the notebook, strode out to his truck, and came back in with two evidence bags. Sealed the book in the bag and wrote down the required information. He then put the cash back into the makeup bag and repeated the process.

"Ten thousand dollars." He wrote the number on the bag. "Where would she get that kind of cash?"

"I don't know." I shrugged.

Things were beginning to come together in my head, but I didn't want to say anything to Nate until I was sure.

I went back into the bedroom, gathered up the clothes for Adrianna, and put them in the bag Nate had provided. By the time I got back out into the living room, the crime scene techs were there, and gave me a weird look when I came out of the bedroom with an evidence bag. Nate explained the situation to them.

"I should go," I said. "I have to get these to David at the funeral home."

"Dinner later?" he said.

"Sure."

"I'll pick you up at six." He gave me a quick kiss at the door.

When I got home, Atlas bounded up to the door and gave me a rowdy greeting. Karma meowed her displeasure at being disturbed. I'd been really busy lately, and felt bad that I hadn't spent a lot of time with them.

While Atlas ran around in the backyard, I gave Karma a few treats, which seemed to mollify her cranky mood.

I searched the house, but couldn't find Adrianna's key anywhere. *What the hell?*

Atlas got a treat when he came in, and then I grabbed my cell phone and headed for my office. If my hunch was right, I should have confirmation within seconds.

I opened the picture of Adrianna and ran it through an image search. When the results popped up on my screen, I almost vomited. She had been an escort—and a high-priced one at that. Her online persona was Gracey Merlot, which is why it never popped up in any of my research. She'd worked for an escort service in Detroit. The pictures of her on the website, in her sexy lingerie, were too much for me to bear, and I closed the website.

It all made sense—the designer clothes, fancy underwear, the book with the initials and other information.

Adrianna had been a high-class hooker.

26

Just as I reached for my cell phone to tell Nate about Adrianna being a call girl, my doorbell rang and sent Atlas into a frenzy. He was barking, whining, and wagging his tail so hard I thought he was going to knock himself over.

When I opened the door, Frank and Bea were standing on the porch, and I invited them in.

"We're engaged!" Bea held out her hand to show me the vintage diamond ring that adorned her finger.

"Oh, my gosh!" I gave each of them a hug. "I'm so happy for both of you."

Frank was beaming, and he never let his gaze wander too far from Bea.

"I was so nervous," he said. "I thought for sure she was going to turn me down."

"Oh, *pshh.*" Bea kissed his cheek.

"This calls for a celebration!" I walked into the kitchen to open a bottle of wine, and poured three glasses, then handed one to them both. "Sorry it's not champagne."

"This is perfect," Bea said.

We toasted to their engagement.

"So when's the wedding?"

They exchanged glances.

"We're not sure." Bea looked at me. "What would you think of a summer wedding in the park?"

"Perfect. Frank?" I looked at him.

"Whatever she wants is fine with me."

Good answer.

We sat around and chatted for an hour. And when they left, I shut and locked the door behind them.

I was thrilled. Bea and Frank both deserved to be happy, and to have someone. I did, too, but my prospects weren't looking good.

I went back to my office to call Nate.

"She was an escort," I said.

"Yeah, we figured it out. I was just about to call you. This opens up a whole new group of suspects. We're working to decipher her code for the men she met.

"Well, it helps that she wrote down the places she met them, right?" I started to wash out the wine glasses.

"Yes. Some of my team is going to try to get any security footage these places may have. It's going to be a long night. Can we do dinner another time?"

"Of course. I'll just run up to Gil's and grab something. Good luck."

I was disappointed that I'd have to eat alone yet again, but knew it was more important for Nate to track down who Adrianna had been seeing.

I grabbed my bag and set the alarm before heading out for the short walk to Gil's. I was halfway down the street when I heard someone coming up behind me. I whirled around and saw Jason.

"Hey, wait up." He broke into a trot.

I stopped and waited for him.

"Where you going?" he said.

"Dinner," I snapped, and glared up at him, fists at my side. "Why were your fingerprints on the candy box at Adrianna's. And why did you say the candy was for me? You've never bought me a box of candy in your life!"

"Zoey, I can explain." Sadness washed over his face. "Can I buy you dinner?"

I shrugged and started walking. He took a hold of my arm and turned me to face him.

"Zoey, I didn't kill those girls. Please say you believe me." His eyes pleaded.

I stared at him for a long minute. "I believe you didn't kill those girls. But I don't believe for one minute that box of candy was for me."

"I can work with that. Let's go to the Blue Bass."

We walked the rest of the way in silence. When we got to the restaurant, Jason requested a quiet table in the back corner. He pulled my chair out for me and then settled in across the table. We each ordered a glass of wine. I excused myself to use the ladies' room and asked him to watch my purse. A couple minutes later, I returned to the table.

"Listen." He leaned forward over the table. "The candy was for you. I know I've been acting like a real jerk the last few weeks, and I'm sorry."

The waitress delivered our wine.

"So you were going to use the candy to try to apologize?" I took a sip of the wine.

Jason waved the waitress away and told her we'd order in a few minutes.

"Yes. And I was planning a special night to take you out and try to make up for my behavior. But someone broke out the window of my truck and stole the candy. It had to be the same person who killed Adrianna. The poor girl." He shook his head.

"You know she was an escort, right?" I stared at him.

"What?" His eyes flew open wide, and his jaw dropped.

I explained what I'd found out.

"Unbelievable," he said.

"It is." I nodded.

The waitress came back to our table, and we ordered dinner and another glass of wine.

"So what has been going on with you lately?" I said. "Why have you been so mean to me?"

He reached across the table and took my hand. "Because I love you, Zoey."

"Wait! What?" I pulled my hand away. "You've been treating me like crap because you love me? That doesn't even make any sense." I shook my head, sat back in my chair, and folded my arms across my chest.

"Here's the thing." He took a gulp of wine. "I always imagined I'd grow up and marry a woman who wanted to be in a more traditional relationship. You know, the man goes to work. The woman stays home and takes care of the house, the kids, and is involved in her women's groups or whatever."

"Huh? This isn't the 1950s, Jason."

"I know. But that's how my family worked." He shrugged. "I guess it's what I was used to. I wanted that, Zoey. I wanted that so bad."

"Go on."

The waitress delivered our salads, and I dumped the dressing on mine.

"Then I met you. You were different, you know? Independent, impulsive, smart, beautiful."

I smiled.

"And when you said you liked me, I felt like I'd won the lottery. But then you kept putting yourself in danger, and it broke my heart."

"Why?"

"Because if something happened to you, I wouldn't be able to live with myself. I tried everything to discourage you. But nothing worked." He looked into my eyes.

I used my fork to shuffle the lettuce around in the salad bowl.

"But that's who I am, Jason. I'm not going to change. Not for you. Not for anyone."

"I understand that now." He wiped his mouth with a napkin. "I want you back, Zoey. Every time I see you with Nate, I get so jealous I can't stand it."

Before I could respond, the waitress sat our dinners down on the table.

"Jason," I cut into my steak, "you know I care about you. But I need some time to think. You've gone out of your way to make my life difficult lately."

"I understand. At least you didn't shut me down completely." He winked at me and smiled.

We both worked to keep the conversation light while we ate. He told me about how the renovations were going at the Rockford house, and I loved the way his eyes lit up when he talked about it. It seemed more like the Jason I'd fallen in love with.

"The funeral for Adrianna and her father is tomorrow," I said. "Are you coming?

"Yeah, for sure. Can we go together?"

I nodded. "Pick me up at nine. The service is at ten-thirty, but I want to make sure everything is perfect."

"It's a good thing you're doing." He nodded. "You really are an amazing woman."

I felt myself blush. "Thanks."

We finished dinner, and I tucked a couple of bites of steak into my bag as a treat for Atlas. After Jason paid the bill, we started home. As we strolled along, I looped my arm through his and put my head on his shoulder. He made me feel safe. It was one of the things I liked most about him.

He walked me to my door and gave me a soft kiss goodnight. After he left, I let the dog out and gave him and Karma a couple treats. Before letting Atlas back in, I fished through my purse to get the bit of steak for Atlas. Once I pulled the napkin out of my purse, something pinged when it hit the kitchen countertop.

The key to Adrianna's house. *What the hell?* I could have sworn I'd looked everywhere in my bag.

Atlas was barking at the back door, so I slipped the key back into my bag and gave him his treat.

As I got ready for bed, I thought about what Jason had said. I knew I loved him, but I wasn't ready to trust him again. At least, not for a while. Nate was a great guy, but the Boy Scout vibe could get boring after a while. Besides, Nate and I hadn't even talked about entering into a relationship, and I wasn't sure what we had. My guess is that we were just going to be friends. I wondered how Jason would deal with that.

I went to my office and turned on the laptop. While I waited for it to boot up, I pulled out Bea's genealogy file and scanned through it. My mind kept going back to Inspector Martinelli, and why he had arrested Bea's relative.

I did another search to find out more information about Martinelli. But this time I dug deeper. It took a while, but I managed to find an old Ph.D. thesis about the way bureaucracy and organizational structure destroyed police efficiency, on an obscure website that quoted Deputy Chief Inspector Martinelli: *"We have a few suspects in the Jack the Ripper case. Aaron Kosminski, Jacob Levy, and Walter Sickert. We just need to be vigilant, and I truly wish the women who worked in the brothels, or on the street at night, would take this more seriously..."*

Hmm. Could it be that Inspector Martinelli was arresting these women to keep them off the streets, and save their lives?

Being familiar with the Jack the Ripper case, I was surprised by the inclusion of Jacob Levy. But the other two men were generally accepted as main suspects in the Ripper murders. However, this was the first time I'd heard of the London police arresting prostitutes to keep them safe and out of the grisly clutches of Jack the Ripper, and I wasn't sure whether this would be the case in 19th century London. If anyone would know, it would be Professor Frost. I made a note to call him in the morning.

I continued working on other branches of Bea's family for a couple more hours, and the chances of finding royalty in her great-grandmother's line that came from France was looking promising.

Knowing I had a big day tomorrow, I shut down my computer, locked up my file cabinets, and headed for my room. As I crawled into bed with Atlas and Karma, I thought about Adrianna and her father's funeral tomorrow, and I found myself dreading it.

27

When I got out of the shower in the morning, I called Professor Frost—told him I had a few questions, and asked if we could get together in the next couple days. He was his usual charming self, and said he was distressed when he'd heard about Adrianna's death. We set up a time and day to meet.

I wore the same outfit to Adrianna's funeral as I wore to my Uncle Felix's. I was tempted to wear my little black dress, but it was too short for a funeral.

Jason rang the doorbell earlier than I would have liked, but he looked handsome in his black suit, pale purple shirt, and black tie.

"Give me five minutes," I said, when I opened the door.

He rolled his eyes and started playing with Atlas.

I ran back to my bedroom to put in my earrings, then slipped into my shoes and grabbed my black clutch.

Jason gave me an approving look when I came back into the living room. He helped me put my jacket on, and we left for the funeral home.

I was glad we got there early, because I wanted to spend a few minutes alone with Adrianna. My head wanted to scream at her for lying and concealing facts that may have kept her alive. But my heart was filled with sadness. I stood in front of her casket and stared at her face. She looked angelic.

Jason came up beside me and pulled a white rose from the flowers draped over her casket. He snapped off the long stem, which had thorns, and placed the flower in her hands. It amazed me that such a simple gesture reflected his compassion and kindness. I stood on my tiptoes and kissed his cheek.

"What was that for?" He looked at me.

"For being you." I turned around to greet the mourners who were beginning to show up.

Adrianna's father's casket was closed, of course, but I had still purchased flowers to go on top of it, and had framed a picture of the man he used to be.

I was surprised to see that many of the townsfolk had come to pay their respects for people they didn't even know. It touched my heart.

Agent Phillips, Nate, and Bea all approached the caskets separately to pay their respects.

Father Alexander came in, and we had a short, but meaningful, ceremony for father and daughter. I hadn't planned a wake. I just didn't see the point. But Bea and the women's group from St. Agatha's had put together a small luncheon in the community center.

When the service was over, I tried to beg off from having to go to the luncheon, but Bea wouldn't hear of it. I grabbed a croissant filled with tuna salad, and tried to disappear into a corner, but to no avail.

Two hours later, I begged Jason to take me home, and we went out to his truck. He opened the door for me, and we drove back to my house. He let the dog out while I changed clothes, and I rejoined him at the kitchen island.

He left a while later, and I was glad for the time alone so I could get to work on the badly neglected FBI files, before going to bed.

Sunday rolled around, and I felt like a slug. I even neglected to go for a run. I didn't want to do much of anything, so I cleaned the house and spent time chilling with Karma and Atlas. We watched old movies, and just enjoyed a quiet and relaxing day.

I pulled out the information I'd need for tomorrow's meeting with Professor Frost. Bea's paperwork had grown considerably, so I transferred all of it into a red rope accordion file folder, before crawling into bed.

***

I spent the entire day working on the FBI files, and had been productive. I'd identified another Jane Doe, and prepared the report for Agent Phillips before I shut everything down around six so I could get ready for my meeting with Professor Frost.

I made it to Gil's with three minutes to spare. The professor was settled into a booth close to the front of the restaurant, and he stood to greet me when he saw me come through the door.

"I took the liberty of ordering you a glass of wine," he said, as I sat, and nodded toward the glass in front of me.

"Thank you."

He was impeccably dressed, as usual, and looked comfortable in the surroundings.

"So my dear, what seems to be the problem you're having?"

I took a sip of my wine, then opened up the large file I'd brought with me, and withdrew a folder.

"I was curious. I found an article that said the police were arresting prostitutes to keep them safe from Jack the Ripper? Would that have been true?" I looked up at him.

He chuckled. "I've heard that theory before. But most people dismiss it. In my humble opinion, the police were using the Ripper murders as an excuse to clean up the Whitechapel area of London."

"I see. Well, that explains that."

The professor's explanation seemed more logical than arresting women to keep them safe.

We ordered dinner, and before it arrived, I excused myself to use the restroom. By the time I got back to the table, my chef's salad was waiting for me. While we ate, we had a good discussion on the Jack the Ripper case, and voiced our own theories.

"What I find most curious about the Ripper case is that Jacob Levy was a suspect at all." I looked at him.

"Oh, yes, Jacob." The professor scowled, and his voice took on a bitter tone. "Inspector Martinelli hounded that poor man."

I chuckled. "Well, I guess that's what detectives do. They apparently had some type of evidence against him."

"Rubbish! Jacob was a respectable butcher with a wife and six children, for God's sake." He slammed his fist down on the table.

"Well, there have been quite a few killers with families and ordinary occupations. I can't see that him having a family would exclude him."

"The poor man must have been so distraught. He died of syphilis soon after. His wife and kids struggled after that, of course."

"Sad."

Academics. They think they know it all, and believe no one should dare argue with their knowledge.

"Not just sad, Miss Calloway." The professor frowned. "Tragic. Because of Martinelli's actions, the poverty and shame that befell that family was felt for generations."

"How could that be? I mean, really, Professor. Yes, it was a sad situation. And I'm sure you're more knowledgeable about that era in London than I am. But look at the circumstances."

"Meaning?" He glared at me.

"Meaning, women were being slaughtered. The police were doing everything they could, without the modern forensics we have today. I'm sure many others fell under suspicion as well." I shrugged.

"Perhaps." He stiffened. "But Martinelli's behavior was reprehensible."

Before I could respond, he dropped some money on the table and stood.

"I really must go. I thought this was supposed to be about your fat friend's ancestor. If all you intend to do is defend Martinelli when you are ignorant of the true facts of the case, then please do not call me again. Good night." He stormed out of the restaurant.

I sat there, stunned. *What the hell just happened?* His reaction to Jacob Levy's name seemed out of whack. Probably because he thinks he's the be all and end all to the Jack the Ripper case.

As I munched my salad, curiosity got the best of me, and I pulled my laptop out of my bag. Yep, Jacob Levy, six kids. He got that right. The two sons married—one without issue, the other had a child who died at six.

Hmm. Might have been the result of syphilis.

The only line that flourished was of the youngest daughter, Margaret. She married late for that era. She was twenty-six when she married Samuel Frost.

Frost! Hang on there, Zoey.

I traced the line down—Margaret had a son Bernard, who had a son named…uh-huh…Rodger Ambrose Frost. Born 1961. Professor Frost was the great-grandson of Jacob Levy. No wonder he took the matter personally.

But how personally?

Then everything clicked into place in my head.

I gathered my things, paid the bill, and hurried out into the darkness. I called Nate to tell him what I'd found out, and told him to meet me at my house.

I heard someone come up behind me, but before I could react, I felt the muzzle of a gun dig into the small of my back.

"Walk," Professor Frost said.

He forced me to walk back toward town, and we ducked down a dark alley behind the buildings on Main Street. We turned up a side street, and I found that we were at Adrianna's house.

Professor Frost ripped the bag off my shoulder and pushed it into my hands.

"Get Adrianna's key out of your purse and unlock the door."

We entered the house, and the professor locked the door behind us.

He grabbed the bag out of my hand and dropped it on the kitchen counter.

I looked around the room. The curtains were drawn, and only the dim light on the range hood illuminated the kitchen and living room. Maybe I could use the dark corners to my advantage.

"Why?" I said. "I don't understand."

"Don't you have pride in your heritage?" He glared at me. "Inspector Martinelli ruined my family."

"That was over a hundred years ago."

I glanced around the living room for something I could use as a weapon.

Boy, did I peg Professor Frost wrong. He's a complete nutcase. I need to buy some time.

"And our family still hasn't recovered! He wiped out the family fortune. Jacob Levy was a successful businessman. When word got out that he was a suspect in the Ripper murders, it destroyed him."

"Oh, no wonder you're angry. Martinelli did a disgraceful thing. How many of his family line did you have to get rid of?

He grabbed my arm and forced me into one of the chairs in the living room.

"I tried to warn Adrianna and her pitiful father, but they didn't listen. They didn't understand." A hint of regret in his voice. "I sent them notes. I left them messages. Nothing worked."

"What did you expect them to do? I'm pretty sure they knew nothing of Inspector Martinelli."

"All they had to do was apologize," he whined, like a petulant child. "They just had to say they were sorry."

As much as I wanted to scream at him, I knew if I did, it would only make him angrier.

"It must have been so hard on you and your family living with the stigma."

He crouched down and put his hand on my knee.

"It was! You do understand. The shame and guilt I felt growing up was unbearable."

I put my hand over his. "I'm so sorry that happened to you. So you killed Adrianna and her father?"

"I had to avenge Jacob's unfair persecution, and the persecution our family has been forced to endure since." He looked at me with a pleading expression. "It was the only right thing to do."

"I see. So those other two girls were mixed up in this, too?"

"Yes!" He got to his feet. "They were everything. It was the only way I could think of to convince Adrianna I was serious. But she was a stupid girl and didn't make the connection." He shook his head. "Then, in a weird twist of fate, she turned to being an escort. Only fitting, don't you think? Her ancestor, Chief Martinelli, arrested women like her. I did the world a favor. She was a selfish, vain girl who turned into nothing but a cheap hooker."

I went to say something, but couldn't.

"Professor, you really don't want to kill me, do you? Why don't you put the gun down, and let's get you some help."

"You're right. I don't want to kill you." Regret filled his voice. "But don't you see? You're the only one who knows. I have to. Now that my work is done, I can go back to England, vindicated." His eyes took on a far-away look as he thought about his return home.

My gaze darted to the glass swan statue on the coffee table. I leapt out of the chair and grabbed the statue. But I wasn't fast enough. A shot rang out, and I felt a bullet graze my arm. I dropped the statue and ran toward the hallway leading to Adrianna's bedroom, pausing only long enough to grab my bag off the kitchen counter.

Another shot rang out, and the bullet got lodged into the wall next to my head. When I reached Adrianna's room, I hid behind the bedroom door.

"Zoey, it's really no use to prolong this."

His voice was close. *He must be heading toward me.*

I grabbed the laptop out of my purse and let the bag fall to the floor. In the distance, I heard police sirens.

When the professor came into the bedroom, I raised my laptop and hit him over the head. He crumpled to the floor. I sidestepped his body and raced for the front door. When I swung it open, Nate and two policemen were running up the steps to the front porch.

I threw myself into Nate's arms, and everything went dark.

EPILOGUE

When I woke up in the hospital, Nate, Jason, and Bea were there. Turns out, when the professor shot me, the bullet got lodged in my arm, and didn't just graze me, like I'd thought.

The doctor said recovery was going to be a little longer than normal because of the bullet breaking a bone. Surgery to remove it had been successful. The rest was up to me and a physical therapist. *Peachy.*

Bea said not to worry, that Atlas and Karma were at her house being spoiled rotten, and she was thrilled to have them. That's Bea—always needs someone to look after or take care of. I loved her for that.

Two days later, I checked myself out of the hospital and had Shannon take me home. My laptop was ruined, so on the way home from the hospital, Shannon agreed to stop at a computer store so I could get a new one.

When I got home, she went next door to retrieve the animals, but only came back with Karma. Bea thought Atlas would be too much for me to handle for a bit, and thought it was best if he stayed with her for a while. I couldn't argue with her reasoning. Atlas was high-energy, and given how tired and sore I was, it was best he stayed there.

As for Professor Frost, he was cooling his heels in jail until his trial for the murders of Adrianna, her father, and the other poor women who'd been used as pawns in his sick game. I couldn't wait to testify against him.

When the time came, I looked him right in the eye the entire time I was on the witness stand. As much as Adrianna had lied and been a part of an unsavory industry, she didn't deserve to be murdered any more than the other innocent lives he'd taken in his quest for revenge.

Professor Frost was sentenced to four life sentences with no possibility of parole. His so-called triumphant return to England would never happen—except in his dreams.

After I testified, I walked past him and he reached out and grabbed my wrist. I winced in pain, as it was the arm he'd shot me in.

"This isn't over," he said.

I remembered looking down at him. Instead of the noble and dignified man I'd met at the genealogy lecture, he looked like a caged animal. His eyes were wide with panic, and he'd lost weight.

Nate, Jason, and the bailiff started to come to my aid, but I waved them off.

"Adrianna can rest in peace now. She has been vindicated." I pulled my wrist out of his grasp and held my head up high as I walked out of the courtroom.

Agent Phillips told me to take as much time as I needed off work, with pay, so I could heal properly. I didn't even put up a fight. During my downtime, I finished Bea's family tree. Turns out, she did descend from royalty, but in France. One of her extremely distant relatives had been a duke. She'd been thrilled, and according to her triumphant account, she'd put her friend in the mahjong group in her place.

Jason spent as much time as he could taking care of me and driving me to and from my physical therapy appointments. He was putting in a lot of effort to get me back, but I wasn't ready to let him get that close to me again. Maybe sometime in the future. I just couldn't trust him not to become controlling again.

Nate and I remain friends, and casually date. He's a great guy, but I don't know if he's the guy for me.

Only time will tell.

COMING SOON

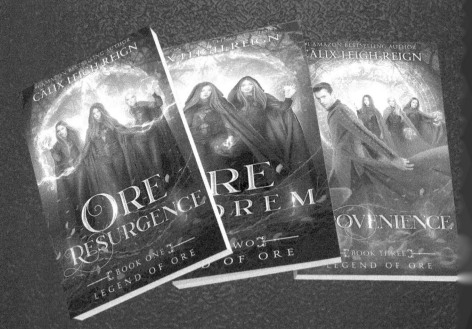

amazon.com

SHOP BOOKS

CayellePublishing.com

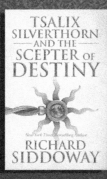

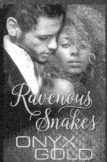

CPSIA information can be obtained
at www.ICGtesting.com
Printed in the USA
FSHW010220100921
84596FS